'No!' she cried on a sudden note of panic, and backed a step from him.

On the instant, as if she were a hot coal, his hands dropped away from her. 'It's all right! I won't harm you!' Ven swiftly reassured her. He stated evenly, 'Despite how it looks, Fabia, I didn't bring you to Prague to seduce you. . .'

Dear Reader

Dobrý den! Jessica Steele's latest Euromance travels to the very heart of Europe, to the delights of Mariánské Lázně spa with its beautiful landscaped gardens, and to the fairytale city of Prague. The country that was Czechoslovakia has now divided into the Czech Republic and Slovakia, but as the book was written and printed before the so-called 'velvet divorce' please note that it will refer throughout to the country as it was in 1992. *Sbohem*!

The Editor

The author says:

'I arrived in Czechoslovakia and instantly knew I was going to like it. I divided my time there between Prague and the west of the country.

Prague has so much to recommend it: superb buildings and structures—the Charles Bridge and the fascinating astronomical clock to mention just two.

But for me, Mariánské Lázně, in the west of Bohemia, was somewhere very special. Here there is a feeling of space which at the same time mingles well with stately European architecture.

I have since stayed overnight in Prague en route elsewhere, but particularly hope to one day visit Mariánské Lázně again.'

Jessica Steele

★ TURN TO THE BACK PAGES OF THIS BOOK FOR *WELCOME TO EUROPE*. . .OUR FASCINATING FACT-FILE ★

WEST OF BOHEMIA

BY
JESSICA STEELE

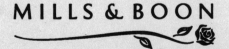

MILLS & BOON

MILLS & BOON LIMITED
ETON HOUSE, 18–24 PARADISE ROAD
RICHMOND, SURREY, TW9 1SR

First published in Great Britain 1993
by Mills & Boon Limited

© Jessica Steele 1993

Australian copyright 1993
Philippine copyright 1993
This edition 1993

ISBN 0 263 78295 6

Set in 10 on 11 pt Linotron Times
01-9312-59484

Typeset in Great Britain by Centracet, Cambridge
Made and printed in Great Britain

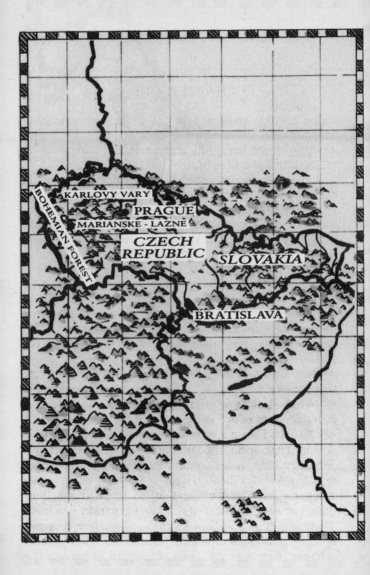

CHAPTER ONE

FABIA stirred, awakened in her hotel bedroom that Monday and, as memory awakened with her, she abruptly closed her lovely green eyes and wished for a moment that she were back in England.

A second or so later she was giving herself a mental shake and opening her eyes again. What she should be doing was looking on the bright side. The only trouble there though, she realised, as despondency tried to set in again, was that, apart from actually being in the delightful spa town of Mariánské Lázně, and actually being here in Czechoslovakia, a country she had wanted to visit, there was no other bright side.

She must have been mad, totally and ridiculously mad, she thought, to have let her sister talk her into making this trip, alone. Not that, given the same set of circumstances, she could see how Cara would have fared any better.

True, Cara was more worldly-wise than she was, but then, at twenty-eight, six years older, you'd expect her to be. And anyhow, Cara would probably not have lasted more than two minutes in her job in the journalistic field had she not grown a few hard edges.

Hard edge or no, though, Fabia was quick to defend her sister even in her solitary thoughts. Cara had one very big Achilles' heel—Barnaby Stewart. Barney was a super person and brilliant at his scientist job, but otherwise a trifle absent-minded and generally helpless. There were times, Fabia well knew, when Barney drove her tidy and efficient compartmentalised sister to distraction. But, just the same, Cara had fallen wholeheartedly in love with him, and a year ago she had married him.

Fabia reached over to the bedside table for her watch. It was early yet, she noted, and, feeling in no hurry to start a day that might well fall into the same luckless category as yesterday and the day before *and* the day before that, she sat up and leant against the headboard.

Events, she mused glumly, had not gone as planned. Oh, how she wished that Cara were here! She should have been, would have been, indeed, originally it had been Cara and not her who had been going to make the trip to Czechoslovakia alone.

Without her realising it, Fabia's thoughts drifted back to the Gloucestershire home she shared with her parents in the village of Hawk Lacey. Her parents ran a smallholding which they combined with a facility for boarding dogs while their owners went away on holiday. Fabia had a soft spot for dogs, and cats too, for that matter, and there had been talk of her training to be a vet. She had been studying for her A levels however when, after discovering that she had smuggled a pining and off-his-food spaniel up to her bedroom to sleep one night, her father had put some of her own recent doubts into words.

'I know someone has to do it, love,' he stated sensitively, 'but I'm not sure that you're cut out to handle the sad side of a vet's business.'

'You wouldn't feel that I was letting you down if I didn't go to veterinary college?' she asked — and felt the happiest she had done in weeks at his reply.

'Silly sausage,' he teased, and, although she carried on studying to complete her A levels, when Fabia left school she seemed to just naturally fill the niche that was tailor-made for her in feeding and exercising the dogs and giving an extra helping of love and attention to the animals who needed it.

Her sister was fond of animals too, but had never had very much to do with them and had moved away from home just after her eighteenth birthday. Now that Cara was married, she and Barney lived in London, but Cara came back to Hawk Lacey whenever she could. Sometimes Barney came with her but, because she could sometimes fit in a visit to coincide with when she had work in that area, she sometimes came alone.

It was on one such time early last February, two months ago, when, having driven to Cheltenham to do an interview, she detoured to call in. Fabia couldn't help picking up the air of excitement about her, and realised that she wasn't the only one when barely had they sat down with a cup of tea than her father, an observant man, was asking, 'Are you going to tell us about it — or is it a secret?'

'Guess who's. . .' Cara began.

'You're having a baby!' her mother, longing for a grandchild, joyously mis-guessed.

'*Mother*!' Cara exclaimed exasperatedly. 'I've got enough to do now coping with an exacting career and tidying up after Barney without *adding* to my workload!'

It was a sore point with Norma Kingsdale that her elder daughter had no intention of giving up her career *if* and *when* she decided to start a family. But, as they hadn't seen Cara since Christmas, and it could be another five weeks, or more, since they saw her again, in the interests of enjoying this short while with her she held her peace, and prompted, 'You said "Guess who's. . .".'

Cara needed no more prompting and her eyes had begun to shine again with excitement. 'Guess who's just pulled off the interview of the year?'

After some long while of freelancing, Cara was now working for the superior bi-monthly magazine *Verity*. To Fabia, who thought the world of her, this latest

interview was further proof of how good at her job
Cara was.

'The one you've just done in Cheltenham?' she
asked, catching Cara's excitement as she waited expectantly for her to go on with more details.

But, 'Grief, no!' Cara denied. 'That interview's small
fry compared to this!'

'Oh — so this is an interview you haven't done yet?'
Godfrey Kingsdale queried.

Cara nodded, and elatedly went on to tell them that
she had heard, only that morning when she'd looked in
at her office to check her post before driving up to
Cheltenham, that she'd pulled off an interview with
none other than Vendelin Gajdusek.

'The Czech writer?' Fabia asked. Although she had
never read any of his books, she was well aware of the
high regard he was held in in the literary world.

'The very same!' Cara chortled. 'I can hardly believe
it. I'm still pinching myself to see if I'm awake or
dreaming.'

'But — I thought he never gave interviews?' Godfrey
Kingsdale recalled.

'He doesn't,' Cara agreed, 'which is why it's even
more fantastic that after weeks and weeks of my
buttering up his secretary I've eventually pulled it off. I
still can't believe it — even now when I've got the letter
to prove it!'

A few minutes passed as they congratulated Cara on
what they realised was something of a very large
achievement. Then Mrs Kingsdale asked, 'Will you
have to go to his hotel to do the interview?'

'Hotel?' Cara queried, but as she quickly caught on,
'Oh he's not coming to England — I'm to go to
Czechoslovakia.'

'Czechoslovakia!' her mother exclaimed.

'It's in Eastern Europe, Mum, not Mars,' Cara

laughed, clearly still on a high from her morning's news.

'But—doesn't Barney mind you going?' Norma Kingsdale enquired.

'Barney's as thrilled as I am,' Cara replied, revealing that she had phoned him as soon as she'd read her mail. 'And no, Mother, he doesn't mind. As long as I'm happy in my career, he's all for it.' She smiled then to soften any hint that she was annoyed that her mother thought she should be more home-orientated than she was now that she was married. 'Anyhow, since the earliest Mr Gajdusek will see me is the first week in April, it couldn't have worked out better.'

'Isn't Barney due to fly to the States at the end of March?' Fabia chipped in.

'You've remembered.' Cara smiled, and confided, 'Actually, I was wondering what I was going to do with myself the four weeks he's away—I've sort of got used to having him around,' she tossed in, as if uncaring, when they all knew differently. 'I've now arranged to fly out and spend the last two weeks of his working trip with him as a kind of nosing-around holiday while I'm about it, but the first two weeks. . .' She broke off, then looked to Fabia. 'I say, I've just had the most marvellous idea—why don't you come to Czechoslovakia with me?'

'You don't mean it!' Fabia exclaimed, instantly very much taken with the idea.

'Of course I do,' Cara responded. 'You'd be great company for me, and you'd just love it, I know you would.'

'You're remembering how, when all the other teen-agers were driving their parents barmy with pop music, Fabia blasted us with the music of Smetana, Janáček and Dvořák morning, noon and night,' her father chipped in drily.

'Gross exaggeration,' Fabia laughed, but couldn't

deny that she had been a great fan of the Czech composers, and still was.

'Well?' Cara asked, and Fabia needed no more prompting to turn to her parents.

'Can you manage without me?' she asked.

'You're more than due a holiday,' her mother at once declared.

While her father stated, 'We can easily cope for a week,' and with a questioning look to Cara, 'or two?' he queried.

'Mr Gajdusek lives in the part of Czechoslovakia called Western Bohemia, and I was going to make it a quick flight over, find this place called Mariánské Lázně where he has his home, and shoot back to England again,' Cara replied. 'But if Fabia comes with me we could travel by car, take the ferry across to Belgium and belt through Germany and. . .' At her father's sharp look she broke off. 'We could share the driving and drive sedately through Germany,' she amended with a smirk of a glance to where Fabia was grinning, 'and once I've done my interview we could make a holiday of it — stay longer, have a tour around. We might even take in Prague.'

'Could we?' Fabia asked enthusiastically — and so it was settled.

In the two months remaining Fabia got her cases packed and repacked and purchased a Czechoslovakian-English phrase book. When her father formed the view that the car he and her mother had bought her for her eighteenth birthday was more road-worthy than Cara's outwardly smart but inwardly not so clever vehicle, it was decided that they would use her regularly serviced Volkswagen Polo for the trip.

Fabia and Cara were frequently on the phone to each other in the meantime. But while Fabia's feeling of excitement grew and grew at the prospect of seeing the country of her composer heroes at first hand, her sister's excitement that she was actually going to interview Vendelin Gajdusek grew too. It was as though she still couldn't believe her good fortune that she, out of all those top-notch journalists after an interview with him, had been the one he had agreed to see. Clearly, this was the pinnacle of her career!

By the time the week rolled around when she and Cara would start their trip, Fabia, who had managed to get hold of and read one of Venedelin Gajdusek's translated works, was feeling as much in awe of the man as her sister. While she preferred her reading matter to have a softer edge, she could not but admire the Czechoslovakian writer's sharp cut and thrust of narrative.

It would have been a particular thrill to have met the man who could pen such material, she mused as she closed the lid on her suitcase for the last time on Tuesday morning, but she knew that that was out of the question. The first few days of what she and Cara now termed their 'Czechoslovakian Experience' had been carefully planned, so that Fabia knew in advance that she would never get to see Vendelin Gajdusek.

Again she went over the first few days of their itinerary in her mind. Barney had flown to the States last Thursday, and she was driving to London later that Tuesday to the flat where he and Cara lived. From there, Cara had it all meticulously mapped out: she and Cara were to motor down to Dover to take a ferry to Ostend early on Wednesday morning. Once there they would journey across Belgium and drive 'sedately' on far into Germany where they would rest overnight. On Thursday they would continue through the remainder of Germany and over the Czechoslovakian border. According to Cara, who had accommodation already reserved for them in a hotel in Mariánské Lázně, they should reach their destination by about mid-afternoon. Plenty of time, she had declared, in which for her to catch her breath before, at some time prior to eleven, she went off to keep her highly valued appointment with Mr Gajdusek on Friday morning. After that—it would be holiday time.

Fabia's head was full of the 'Czechoslovakian Experience' in front of her when she stood by her car saying goodbye to her parents.

'Now you'll be sure to. . .'

'Don't worry, Mum,' Fabia beamed to her slightly apprehensive-looking parent. 'You know Cara, she's the last word in efficiency—nothing can go wrong.'

Only a few hours later and Fabia was wishing with all she had that she had touched wood when she'd made that statement. For something *had* gone wrong. Terribly wrong, and that was before they had even left England!

Happy, smiling, confident, she had cheerfully tucked a stray strand of her long pale gold hair behind her ear as she waited for her sister to answer her ring at her doorbell.

The smile on her sweet mouth quickly faded though the moment the door was opened and she at once took in the unusual pallor of Cara's skin and the fact that, if she wasn't mistaken, her dear sister had recently been crying.

'Cara! Love! What's the matter?' she hurried into the flat with her.

'I can't go!' Cara blurted out bluntly.

Fabia was shaken, but was more intent then on finding out what she could do to help whatever the trouble was, than concerned that it looked as though she could say goodbye to her much looked forward to Czechoslovakian holiday. 'Why?' she asked. 'What's happened?'

'Barney—he's ill,' Cara answered but, while plainly still in an emotional state, clearly having shed tears initially, she was now back in charge of herself.

'Oh, no! Oh, love!' Fabia crooned, and putting an arm about her sister, sat down on the settee with her. 'What's wrong with him?' she asked, praying with all she had that it wasn't serious.

'They don't know yet. I had a phone call about three quarters of an hour ago. He's contracted some virus and is half off his head with delirium while the doctors are fighting like mad to find out what it is.'

'You're going to him?' It was more of a statement than a question.

'I rang the airport straight away—they've booked me on the first flight out. Can you take me to the airport? I feel a bit too stewed-up to drive myself,' Cara confessed.

'Of course I'll take you,' Fabia replied without hesitation, and was about to add that she would be on the same flight with her when she was halted by a change in Cara's expression. Knowing her sister well, Fabia could only marvel then that when Barney was, by the sound of it, so desperately ill, Cara appeared to be making every effort to rise above the shocking news she had received less than an hour ago.

She marvelled even more though when Cara's basic efficiency surfaced as she declared, 'By my calculations you'll still have time to get down to Dover after you've dropped me off at the airport.' And, going on in the same vein before Fabia could gently state that she wouldn't dream of going to Czechoslovakia without her, 'It's about a four-hour crossing so you'll have time for some shut-eye and a rest before. . .' Cara broke off, but she was still it seemed trying to frantically keep her mind off how ill her beloved husband might be when, turning the conversation to her work, 'It's a perfect beast that I've got to forgo my interview with Vendelin Gajdusek.' She gave a shaky sigh. 'It was the interview of a lifetime.'

Fabia had forgotten all about Cara's eleven o'clock Friday appointment for the moment, but truly sympath-

ised with her. 'I'm so sorry,' she said gently, well aware
of how much it meant to her. She could therefore only
love her sister more that, when it came to choosing
between this most important interview of her career or
flying to her husband's bedside, Cara wasn't hesitating
to fly to where love and instinct guided. But, as tears
pricked the back of Fabia's eyes, she realised that she
was in danger of becoming over-emotional — which
would be of no help just now to Cara. So, swallowing
hard on her emotion, she strove to be a more practical
help. 'Perhaps,' she suggested tentatively, 'somebody
else — could do this interview for you.'

Cara turned to her, and it was so good to see her
brave smile when she responded, 'They can actually.'
Fabia found an answering encouraging smile, but her
smile did not remain for long when after a second or
two of studying her Cara stated, quite clearly, 'You.'

'*Me*!' Fabia exclaimed, and just knew, at a time like
this, that her sister wasn't joking.

'You're the obvious person to do it,' Cara, ignoring
that her sister was staring at her in total disbelief, went
on. 'I've had time to think it well and truly through in
what has been the longest three quarters of an hour of
my life between phone call and you getting here — and
it just has to be you. I've already made a list of the
questions you should ask h ——'

'Cara!' Fabia protested, needing most urgently to
stop her now before she went any further. 'I can't do
it!' she had to tell her, and, when her sister's look
suddenly became hostile, 'I'm sure if you wrote to Mr
Gajdusek, or phoned him — or I could do it for you,'
she volunteered hastily, not wanting to be bad friends
with her, now of all times. 'Mr Gajdusek would be
bound to understand. I'm sure he'd agree to a later
date if ——'

'Certainly not!' Cara, hostile still, cut her off. 'I've
sweated blood to get him to agree to see me at all. I'm

not, positively not going to mess things up by telling him I can't make the only date he has offered. Besides which, Milada Pankracova, his secretary, expressly stated in her letter giving me the appointment that her employer had no time or inclination to repeat himself, and that this was the last communication they wanted on the subject. I was just to present myself at the right time on the due date, when he would honour his promise to see me. Only,' Cara broke off, and giving Fabia a hard, unsmiling look, 'in this instance, it won't be me he'll be seeing, but you.'

'But, Cara——' Fabia started to get desperate, well remembering countless times when Cara had some notion stuck in her head and how there was no changing it '——can't you get one of your colleagues at the office to keep the appointment for you? They're professionals and——'

'You must be off your head! I've already explained to you how I've worked myself into the ground setting up the interview. If you think I'm letting go this prize gem I've worked towards for all of my career, so that someone else on *Verity* magazine can put their name to it, you've another——'

'Wouldn't they, in the circumstances, put your name——'

'Hell's teeth, have you got a lot to learn!' Cara chopped her off. But then, all at once, her eyes began to fill with tears, and Fabia's heart went out to her. She had difficulty in keeping her own tears back when Cara asked brokenly, 'Couldn't you do this one thing for me? An hour out of your life—that's all it would be.'

'Oh, Cara,' Fabia cried, and felt she must be the meanest person living. What was an hour out of her life, for goodness' sake?

'I'm not asking you to write up the interview. I can do that when I've got your notes. All I'm asking is that you bring back some relevant facts, answers, for me to

piece together,' Cara stated, her voice all quivery.
'Couldn't you do that for me, love?'

How could she refuse? 'Of course,' Fabia replied,
and from then until it was time for her to drive Cara to
the airport she listened intently to all her sister had to
impart.

By the time they were on their way to the airport,
Fabia had a note of Vendelin Gajdusek's address and
was racking her brains to try and think if there was
anything else she needed to know.

They arrived at the airport with time to spare, and
Fabia gently suggested that Cara might want to telephone their parents about Barney. But, 'I don't think
so,' Cara declined. 'They'll probably be in bed by now
anyhow. If things go really wrong for Barney,' she went
on, a hint of a fracture in her voice, 'I'll be in touch
with them. But meantime you'd be doing me a favour
if you didn't ring them either. They'll only try to talk
you out of going to Czechoslovakia to do this job for
me — you know what they're like.'

'I can't lie to them!' Fabia quickly, if reluctantly in
the light of what Cara must be going through, had to
state.

'You won't have to. As far as they know you're co-
driver on this working holiday. They'll hardly expect
separate cards from the two of us, though since you're
likely to be sending them one it wouldn't hurt to add
my name to yours. And talking of cards,' she went on
quickly as it registered with Fabia that if adding Cara's
name to hers on any card she sent home wasn't lying,
then she didn't know what was, 'you'd better take a
couple of my business cards.' Delving into her bag,
Cara extracted a few cards from her wallet and passed
them over to her, and while Fabia, who knew her sister
went by her maiden name in her job, was looking at the
printed cards that announced 'Cara Kingsdale, *Verity*
magazine', Cara was suggesting, 'Keep those by you

just in case Mr Gajdusek wants proof that you represent *Verity*. Oh!' she exclaimed on suddenly spotting an envelope with a Czechoslovakian stamp on in her bag. 'You'd better have this too. It's the important letter stating the date and time of the interview.'

'Won't Mr Gajdusek be annoyed that it's not a professional journalist coming to interview him?' Fabia asked in all innocence — and was utterly horrified not only at her sister's sudden angry change of expression, but more particularly at her reply.

'Oh, *really*!' she exploded impatiently. 'You can't tell him you're not a professional!' she snapped, and, muttering something that sounded uncomfortably like 'wet behind the ears', 'You've got to pretend that you're me — Cara Kingsdale!' she insisted.

'I can't do *that*!' Fabia gasped, appalled at the very idea.

'For heaven's sake! It's not as if he's ever seen either of us, or is ever likely to again,' Cara hissed, as one or two people turned to look at them. And, her tone suddenly changing completely, 'Would it really hurt you so much to pretend to be me for an hour?' she asked mournfully. And, playing her ace, 'Would you let me down — *now*?'

Fabia drove down to Dover unhappily, not liking herself very much that, instead of being co-operative when Cara had so much else to worry her, she had been a shade obstructive. She tried to cheer up as she drove on to the ferry because — having caved in instantly and completely when Cara had asked 'Would you let me down — *now*?' she had ensured that Cara could fly to Barney certain of one thing, if nothing else: that, her word given, she would not let her down.

The crossing to Ostend was uneventful, with Fabia, when not hoping with all she had that everything would be all right with Barney, trying to come to terms with the fact that, despite having an innate aversion to lies and deception, she had just about agreed to practise both. It had to be a lie to write Cara's name on any card she sent home, didn't it? And what was it but deception that she should present herself at Vendelin Gajdusek's home and allow him to think she was her sister?

Fabia drove through Belgium and into Germany wishing with all she had that it were Saturday and that her interview with the highly esteemed author were over.

She was motoring through Germany, though, when it suddenly dawned on her that she hadn't asked Cara that most fundamental of questions—when was she supposed to return to England?

Because of what had happened, some of her excitement at the thought of seeing Czechoslovakia had ebbed. But she had an idea, from Cara's remark about sending a card home, that her sister fully expected her to stay away the whole fortnight as planned. Was that what Cara wanted her to do? Fabia owned that the idea of getting that interview done—hopefully without making a complete hash of it—and then heading straight back for Ostend had tremendous appeal. On the other hand, something was pulling at her, pulling at her and saying—not yet.

She realised then that she was tired and confused. She gave a quick glance at her watch, put on an hour on the ferry to accommodate the time change, and saw that it had gone six, and that, apart for a stop for petrol and a brief stop in Aachen for a cup of coffee, she had been driving more or less continuously since just after nine that morning.

A short while later she pulled up outside a hotel in the thousand-year-old city of Bamberg. Tomorrow she would motor on through the German and the Czechoslovakian borders to her destination in Mariánské Lázně. For today, she'd had it.

Fabia awakened in her hotel room in Bamberg and thought that, had Cara been with her, since their destination was not so very far away now, they would have taken time out to have a look round. She would have liked to take a look at the city's cathedral square on which Castrum Babenberg, the castle of Bamberg, had once stood. But her sister was not with her, and while Fabia prayed again that Barney would be all right, she felt on edge, and a need to get moving.

Pausing only to once more fill up with petrol, she drove through the German border and six miles on stopped at Cheb, on the Czechoslovakian border, where she changed some English pounds for Czech crowns, and drove on wondering if this 'on edge' feeling was going to stay with her until lunchtime tomorrow. By then she should have answers to all the questions Cara had listed, and could then sit back and take one very relieved breath.

Matters, unfortunately, did not quite work out that way. That was to say, up to a point everything went smoothly. She arrived at her hotel in Mariánské Lázně early on Thursday afternoon, where she had a snack in her room while she got out Cara's list and memorised again all the questions she was to put to Mr Vendelin Gajdusek in the morning. Then, still feeling uptight, she left the hotel and took a brief walk down Hlavní Třída, the main street. But she could not lose her anxiety and, finding a guilty conscience the very devil to live with, she returned to her hotel hoping that she would never again be called upon to impersonate her sister.

She was not particularly hungry, but she went down to the hotel's dining-room around eight that evening, then returned to her room to spend a fitful night.

The next morning, from her hotel in the Slavkoský Forest area, she looked out of her bedroom window at the tree-filled hills that surrounded Mariánské Lázně, and had no appetite then either. After some coffee and a yoghurt, she left the restaurant to ask at the desk for directions to Mr Gajdusek's house. From there she returned to her room until, leaving herself plenty of time to spare, and dressed in her best suit, a leaf-green wool affair with a rounded neck and long-line jacket, she ran a final comb through her shining pale gold hair and left the hotel for an address which she had learned was actually on the outskirts of Mariánské Lázně.

But by then she was so inwardly tense at the deception which through love and loyalty she had to perform that she barely noticed the grand buildings as she drove up out of the valley to where the town ended and a tarmacked road through woodland began.

It was in the woodlanded area that a minor road forked left, and it was this road that, as instructed, she steered into. At the end of the road she had to make a right turn when, a few hundred yards later, she came across the most elegant four-storeyed building. This she knew, was where the man she had come to interview lived.

She checked her watch, her insides in a terrible state. She just wasn't cut out for this sort of thing! That was doubly endorsed for her as a feeling of nausea entered the fray of ragged nerves, and she realised that she was fifteen minutes early.

However, outwardly cool, calm and composed, and trying to use up as many minutes as possible, she slowly got out of her car and, just as slowly, moved to the stout front door of the imposing building.

There, she stamped hard on a bolt of panic that would have her turning swiftly about, and made herself press the porcelain doorbell. It was too late to run away then, though, as she fought desperately for composure by mentally going through Cara's lists of questions,

Fabia discovered that she could not remember one of them!

Then, as her heart leapt into her mouth, she heard someone coming. Had she thought, though, that it would be the man she was there to meet, then Fabia would have been disappointed. For it was not a man at all who pulled back the door, but a well-built lady somewhere in her early fifties.

Fabia pinned a smile to her face nevertheless, as, 'Good morning,' she bade the chunky woman.

'*Dobrý den*,' the woman responded with her own 'Good morning'.

For her sister's sake Fabia kept smiling, though her heart failed her that this lady—be she wife, housekeeper or both—knew no English. Nor, if the enquiring look on her face was anything to go by, had she been informed to expect her.

'My name is Fa. . .—hmn,' she coughed to cover her first mistake—and that was before she got started! 'My name is Cara Kingsdale,' she smiled on, and, when that brought forth no response, she was left with nothing to do but press on. 'I'm here to see Mr Gajdusek,' she added, but, apart from a flicker of recognition at the Gajdusek name, there was little other response either. Which left Fabia racking her brains to think of how next best to get through to the woman. Somehow then she recalled the couple of business cards which Cara had given her and, in the hope that the woman might take her card to the master of the house, she dived into her bag and extracted one from her wallet and extended it to the woman.

Relief flooded in when after a quick glance to the card, which clearly meant nothing to her, the woman politely uttered, '*Prosím za prominutí*,' and disappeared.

Fabia's knowledge of the Czech language was practically non-existent. But since she knew that the Czech

word for 'please' was '*prosím*' she was hoping that the
polite woman's parting phrase had been the equivalent
of an English 'Excuse me, please' while she went away
to hand her card over to Vendelin Gajdusek.

When next Fabia heard footsteps coming in her
direction her heart again gave a nervous flutter. But
when the woman she had given Cara's card to hove into
view her heartbeats steadied, for the person who
accompanied her was not male but was a pinafore-clad
woman of about the same age who, duster in hand, had
obviously been brought away from her cleaning duties.

'Good morning,' the woman offered in very heavily
accented English.

But, whether the woman had been heavily accented
or not, Fabia felt a small let-up in her tension that here
was someone who spoke her own tongue. Her tension
was back in full force a minute or so later, though.
Because, having gone again through her earlier ritual
of introducing herself and stating whom she was there
to see, she had learned, if she had translated the
woman's English correctly, that the man she had an
appointment with—was not there!

'He's out for the moment, do you mean?' Fabia,
speaking slowly, tried for clarification. Then, when she
saw she hadn't made herself understood, she again,
more slowly this time, repeated her question.

She waited a moment and, as she saw light dawn on
the other woman's face, she started to think that they
were getting somewhere. That was until, 'Prague,' the
pinafored woman suddenly announced.

'Prague!' Fabia echoed, and hoped as light dawned
on her that she had got it right, 'You're saying that Mr
Gajdusek is *going* to Prague?'

'He there,' was the unbelievable reply.

'He's there!' Fabia exclaimed, and still didn't want to
believe it, even when the woman vigorously nodded
her head.

'*Ano* — yes,' she translated.

'But — I've an appointment with him!' Fabia protested — and saw that the word appointment was a word the woman didn't understand. Though since to find an alternative word wasn't going to alter matters at all by the look of it, Fabia began to wonder if perhaps Vendelin Gajdusek was coming back from Prague today to keep his appointment but had been delayed for some reason or another. So, changing tack, 'You're expecting Mr Gajdusek today?' she questioned, and when she saw that she wasn't getting through, she pointed to her watch and in pidgin English enquired, 'What time Mr Gajdusek come?' and was incredulous at the answer.

'One week,' the woman informed her.

Ten minutes later Fabia drove away from Vendelin Gajdusek's home feeling disbelieving and stunned. She had pressed the pinafored lady for confirmation that she had understood her last question, but the answer had still come back 'one week'. It was then that, belatedly, Fabia remembered Milada Pankracova with whom her sister had communicated and, 'Mr Gajdusek's secretary?' she enquired.

'Secretary?'

'Milada Pankracova.'

'Ah,' the name obviously registered Fabia thought, her spirits rising. But, 'She gone,' the woman added, and Fabia realised that that must mean that Mr Gajdusek, plainly on business in Prague, had taken his secretary with him. Now what did she do?

What she could do, Fabia realised by the time she was back at her hotel and in the lounge with a cup of coffee, was to return to England without delay. She had tried to do what Cara had asked of her. Indeed, she couldn't have got closer to doing what Cara wanted than to drive up to Vendelin Gajdusek's house at the appointed time and ring his doorbell.

In no hurry now, Fabia sat sipping her coffee. Yes, she decided, she had tried, done her best for Cara, but. . . Annoyingly, other thoughts began to trip her up. Best? Was that really true?

Fabia did not need the nightmare of a conscience just then. But as more unwanted probings prodded, she was set to seriously wonder if indeed it was good enough to have called at Vendelin Gajdusek's home and left it at that. Thoughts of her dear sister and all that she must be going through started to get to her, and, as love and conscience did a double act, she couldn't help thinking that surely she could do more.

She was supposed to be on holiday anyhow, for goodness' sake, so there was absolutely no need at all for her to rush home. And anyhow, when this interview meant so very much to Cara, surely it wouldn't hurt her to hang on in Mariánské Lázně for a week?

Fabia knew that her mind was made up then, even though she couldn't have said with any conviction that she looked forward to going up to that large, elegant house again in a week from now. She had no guarantee that Mr Gajdusek would see her then, of course. But surely, with talk in the letter which Milada Pankracova had sent on his instruction of him honouring his promise, see her he would — or her sister.

Fabia counteracted any feeling of wretchedness at that last guilty thought by deciding that it really wasn't good enough that Vendelin Gajdusek had gone away when he knew full well that someone was travelling especially from England to see him. Agreed, the appointment *had* been made two months ago. And it was quite possible, she supposed, that he or his secretary could have phoned *Verity* magazine in London last Wednesday to leave a message that he had been called away. He wasn't to know that the journalist he was expecting had opted to take the longer route overland rather than to fly out on Thursday.

Realising that her crossness with Vendelin Gajdusek had been short-lived and had quickly faded, Fabia was left to worry about Cara, and Barney, and the interview which by rights should now be over, but which hadn't begun yet. By anybody's reckoning, she still had another week in which to go through agonies about it.

Determinedly, however, Fabia decided she must not think about it. Though that was easier said than done she would do her best, and try instead to enjoy what she could of the coming seven days, and treat each day as a holiday and as if she hadn't a care in the world.

To that end, Fabia left her hotel and, an inveterate walker, explored the highways and byways of Mariánské Lázně. Having stopped a couple of times for refreshment, Fabia returned to her hotel around six o'clock, and realised that she had found Mariánské Lázně quite enchanting.

On Saturday she again walked for some hours around and about the tree-lined, wide, clean streets of the spa town with its artistic colonnade and its many curative springs. She had read how the town formed a part of what was known as the West Bohemian Spa Triangle, the other two being a town called Karlovy Vary and another called Františkovy Lázně.

She strolled by some quite lovely nineteenth-century architecture — charming four-storeyed buildings of white, of yellow, of yellow and white, and red-roofed, green-roofed, immaculately lawned — and down to her hotel. She had five whole days to go yet before she might chance to see Vendelin Gajdusek, she mused and, suddenly fired with enthusiasm, and mobile, she toyed with the idea of taking a look at the other spa towns — if they were not too far distant.

'Can you tell me how far it is to Karlovy Vary and Františkovy Lázně?' she asked the male receptionist when she reached her hotel.

'With pleasure,' the man beamed, making a discreet

meal of her beautiful features and exquisite complexion.

Fabia arose on Sunday morning, thought of Cara, of Barney, and of the man she had never yet met but, with guilty conscience, hoped to, and then attempted to shed her anxieties by remembering that, with Františkovy Lázně being less than twenty-five miles away, Františkovy Lázně was where she was heading for that day.

Shortly after breakfast Fabia nosed her Volkswagen Polo in the direction of that other spa town and fifty minutes later she was walking through the spa park with its trees, benches and bandstand. For an hour or so Fabia wandered around the area which the dramatist Goethe had once called 'a paradise on earth', and began to wish that she had more holiday than she had in which to explore more fully.

She was in the happiest frame of mind she'd known in recent times when later that day she returned to her car. She had gone only a little way however, when she stopped to check her map and, to her consternation found that when she turned the ignition on again her car wouldn't go!

To begin with she just sat there, unable to believe that it wouldn't start. But, when nothing she could do from inside the car would make it go again, she began to realise in her non-mechanical mind that she had something of a problem on her hands.

To get out of the car to peer beneath its bonnet was not going to get her anywhere either, she knew in advance, because with her lack of mechanical knowledge the fault could be staring her in the face and she would never recognise it.

With anxiety uppermost, she flicked an abstracted glance to her rear-view mirror and, oh, grief, she thought, realising only then that the road she was on being more of a lane really, she was stuck bang in the middle of it and there was a sleek black Mercedes sat behind her, patiently waiting to pass.

Knowing that there was nothing for it but to go and apologise and, if possible, explain that her regularly serviced car was misbehaving, Fabia had her hand on the door-handle when she realised that she had no need to move. For from her mirror she saw the driver's door of the Mercedes open and a tall, aristocratic man step out.

Oh, crumbs, she thought, winding her window down as he approached. She had no need to worry about making herself understood, though, she realised, for no sooner had the casually but expensively dressed dark-haired man bent down to the window than in faultless English he was commenting easily, 'Having trouble?'

'It — my car won't go! she said in a hurry, her heart skipping a crazy flustered beat as a pair of intelligent penetrating dark eyes took in her long pale-gold coloured hair, her green eyes, her features and complexion. 'It was going all right, but now it won't go at all,' she added more slowly, as she struggled for composure and it dawned on her that with a GB plate stuck on the back of her car that it wouldn't take a genius to work out that she was probably English.

'You've tried everything, I suppose?' he asked in barely accented, pleasant tones, and earned more of her approval that he wasn't talking down to her.

'Short of lifting up the bonnet. But it wouldn't mean very much to me if I did,' she confessed to the tall lean man whom she assessed as being somewhere in his middle thirties.

'It wouldn't mean very much to me either,' he replied with some charm, and, while Fabia's heart gave a most unexpected flutter, he promptly took charge of her problem and, pointing to a patch of ground a little way over to the right, instructed, 'Steer your car over there.

I'll push you into some sort of position where I can overtake and then tow you to a garage.'

Fabia was still in stunned surprise that her Volkswagen Polo was going to be towed by a Mercedes when the stranger went to the rear of her car and she had to snap out of her shock to steer.

She was still not quite believing any of it when within half an hour her car was safely deposited at a garage. 'Thank you very much for towing me here.' She turned to the stranger who had just finished talking to a mechanic who was now giving her car the once-over. 'I hope I haven't held you up for too long,' she apologised quickly, realising that he could well have an appointment, and that he was on the point of leaving.

But, curiously giving her inordinate pleasure, 'I'm in no great hurry,' he replied, with what she realised was a natural charm. 'I'm on holiday.'

Did he mean that he was on holiday because it was Sunday, or did he mean that he was on holiday in the area? Fabia, although she would have liked to ask that question, knew that they were not well enough acquainted for her to ask, or pass any comment that was more than a surface one.

'Well, thank you anyway,' she said gratefully, and smiled. She was aware of a pair of dark eyes briefly on her mouth, and then the mechanic left her car and came over to them.

While the two men conversed in a language she could not understand, Fabia stood by and hoped that the problem with her car was not a serious one. When the two had finished speaking, she looked expectantly to her tall and charming rescuer.

'The news is not so good, I'm afraid,' he began. 'Your car needs a new alternator.'

'Oh, dear,' Fabia muttered, trying to look intelligent but an alternator meaning nothing to her. But since it seemed that her car was going nowhere without one,

'Could the mechanic fit one for me—as a matter of some urgency?' she asked anxiously—and discovered that her rescuer must have already put that same question to him.

For, 'He could, if he had one in stock for your make of car,' he replied.

Oh, heck, Fabia thought, and for a moment was flummoxed to know what to do next. Somehow she was starting to have an uneasy feeling that alternators for Volkswagon Polos were not too thick on the ground in Czechoslovakia. 'Er—how long would it take him to get the part?' she enquired, fearing the worst.

'It could take quite some days,' the stranger replied.

'I can't have my car back today?' she asked quickly, trying for all she was worth not to panic when he shook his head. How in creation was she to get back to Mariánské Lázně without her car?

But, for all the world as though he had read her mind, her efforts not to panic, 'Where are you staying?' the man questioned.

'Not in Františkovy Lázně,' she replied. 'I've driven this way from Mariánské Lázně.'

The man, she was discovering though charming, was not too free with his smiles. But, he favoured her with what she could only perceive as a reassuring smile when, 'I'm on my way to Mariánské Lázně myself,' he commented easily, 'so that's one problem you can forget.' And while relief surged through her that this kind stranger was, by the look of it, offering to give her a lift back to her hotel, he turned to the mechanic, gave him some instruction and, turning back, informed her, 'They'll get the part as quickly as they can, but in the meantime we will have to leave your vehicle here.'

Fabia was soon seated beside the stranger; in no time his car was gliding speedily and effortlessly along, and in the following half-hour, as they exchanged one or two impersonal comments, Fabia began to recover from her most recent calamity.

But as the car sped on, it was still very much on her mind that with her car lifeless, the garage mechanics the only people able to put some life back into it, she'd had no option but to leave her car back there. It rather put paid to any idea she'd had of motoring around and discovering more of the area though. And she could forget about making a visit to Karlovy Vary, that was for sure. However, with Vendelin Gajdusek out of town and that interview still hanging over her head, a missed trip to the third spa town of the triangle, she inwardly sighed, was the least of her worries!

'You're in Czechoslovakia on holiday?' the stranger suddenly enquired, and Fabia warmed to him. For it seemed to her then that he was aware that her thoughts were troubled and, when he had no need whatsoever to put himself out, he had decided to take her mind off them for a brief while.

'Yes,' she answered.

'Enjoying your trip?'

'Very much,' she replied — well, she had fallen a little in love with Mariánské Lázně, and he was much too sophisticated a man to want to be bored by her problems.

'You're here alone?'

'Oh, yes,' she replied, and because she had almost added that she had been going to travel with her sister — which would surely then have led to her boring him out of his skull with all of the rest of it, 'All alone,' she added with feigned cheerfulness.

'Your parents, they don't mind you being away from home on your own?' he questioned.

'I'm twenty-two!' Fabia declared, stoutly, it somehow not sitting very well at all that he seemed to think of her as a child.

'Forgive me,' he apologised, 'you look younger,' and

at the charm in him, in his voice, Fabia forgave him instantly. 'Did I ask your name?' he enquired, and a smile started somewhere inside her because, at a guess, she'd have said he was a man who forgot nothing.

'You didn't. It's Fabia K. . .' A deer jumping out over a hedgerow and straight in front of the car frightened her half to death before she could finish. By good fortune, not to mention cool-headed driving, neither the deer nor the Mercedes came to grief. 'That was a touch close,' she murmured, as the deer crossed the road and leapt over another hedge and disappeared.

'Is that what they call British understatement?' he asked drolly, as they glided out of countryside and into the outskirts of Mariánské Lázně, and Fabia just had to laugh.

He turned to glance at her as if the sound of her laugh was quite pleasant to his ears. Then asked the name of her hotel, and in no time he was pulling up outside it, and Fabia knew that one of the most pleasant interludes of her life except for the 'alternator' trauma that went with it — was over. That fact that it was over was all there in his formal goodbye when he came round to the passenger's side and stood on the pavement with her, and, '*Na shledanou*, Fabia,' he wished her.

'Thank you so much for your help,' she replied sincerely. But, when she suddenly discovered an urgent desire to know his name, she knew that she would only end up feeling foolish if she asked him what it was in this moment of parting. So, 'Goodbye,' she smiled, and turned into the hotel entrance.

Oddly, thoughts of the stranger haunted her for the rest of that day. He had seemed to be a man who knew his way around. At any rate, he had soon found a garage, and one with a mechanic who worked on a Sunday. And that charm. . .!

Fabia went down to dinner that night and couldn't

help thinking that, even though it was certain that he wasn't staying in the same hotel, or he'd have said so, perhaps he might decide to have his dinner there. There was a good chance that he was in Mariánské Lázně on holiday, wasn't there? It was quite conceivable, too, that he might have thoughts of visiting the Spa Triangle.

Fabia went to bed that night having seen nothing of the man who had given her a lift, but with other more important issues rising to the surface. Yet, while she was finding him most difficult to forget, the realisation only then struck her that she knew neither the name of the garage that housed her car, nor the place where it was situated! Heavens, how in creation was she to phone them to ask if they'd got that part yet?

She slept badly, with what sleep she did get punctuated with dreams where Barney was driving away in her car, and where Cara was blaming her for letting him take it.

All in all, she was glad when morning came. Then, as some car in the street outside her hotel coughed and choked and backfired, Fabia abruptly came out of the long reverie she had fallen into, and back to the present, to realise that it was Monday morning—did she think she was going to sit there in bed all day?

With little enthusiasm for the day, Fabia got out of bed and, mulling over her problems and the fact that anywhere she went from now on would have to be on foot, she pattered to the bathroom to take a shower.

She was under the shower, however, when she thought that, fingers crossed, perhaps there weren't too many garages in, say, a ten-mile radius of Františkovy Lázně. But, even if she did find their name and address, since the alternator needed seemed to be going to take some time to track down, there seemed little point in trying to contact them that day.

Which—she strove to be positive—left her the whole day in which to take her ease in Mariánské Lázně. The problem there though was that, with her mind on the fidget, she didn't feel like taking her ease either.

Very well, dictated that part of her that was against gloom and pushed her again towards the positive, since it was decided that she couldn't do anything that day about the one major problem—her car—how about tackling her other major problem—that interview?

How? she pondered as she made her way down to breakfast. Unless she had misunderstood the pinafore-clad lady up at Vendelin Gajdusek's house, the earliest he was expected back was this Thursday.

Fabia was cutting into a slice of cheese when suddenly she halted. Had she got it wrong? Had she been mistaken? She went over the conversation with the pinafored lady again. She had definitely, most definitely said 'one week'. But then her English wasn't awfully good, was it? Suddenly, Fabia experienced the same familiar churning of inner agitation which appeared every time that interview grew imminent.

For a brief while she toyed with the idea of telephoning Mr Gajdusek's home to check if he was there. Against that, though, was the fact that, if he and his secretary were still away, she stood to have the same unsatisfactory conversation with the lady with a little English as before. And if he and his secretary had returned, she felt she stood a better chance of establishing an interview by calling in person rather than trying to do so over the phone.

She returned to her room, giving herself a talking to along the lines of, what else had she got to do that day anyhow? She had been going to take a walk around Mariánské Lázně, hadn't she, so a three mile walk or so up to Vendelin Gajdusek's home wouldn't be so difficult, would it?

For the next half-hour Fabia battled with conscience, common sense, and an instinctive feeling that she didn't want to do it — and that it would be a wasted exercise anyway.

Five minutes later she had conquered her nerves and made two concrete decisions. One was that, since she was on a fool's errand anyway, she wasn't going to dress up for it. With that in mind, her best suit stayed in the wardrobe, and she opted to cover her long shapely legs in a smart pair of trousers, added a pair of walking shoes, and topped it with a shirt and sweater. The other decision she made was that, on the one-per-cent chance that it wasn't a fool's errand she was on, since it was uphill for most of the way and she didn't want to arrive hot and sticky, she would take a taxi up, and walk down. She rang Reception.

There was a minute to go before ten o'clock when Reception rang her to say that her taxi was here. Accompanied by familiar butterflies, Fabia shrugged into a jacket and left her room. Much before she was ready she was whisked up to Vendelin Gajdusek's home, deposited outside his elegant and graceful house, and, even while she wanted to call the driver back, he was already on his way.

She took a deep and steadying breath, then looked at the house and mentally squared her shoulders. When she was about to move forward though, ready to go up to that front door and ring the bell, some sound drew her attention to the corner of the house. A second later she knew what the sound was, for having heard her too, the most beautiful Dobermann suddenly came tearing round the side of the house and charged full pelt at her.

Only then did Fabia realise how much she had missed the dogs at home, and 'Hello, darling,' she crooned — and for her trouble had the dog whip round her and grip her ankle in its teeth. My mistake, she recognised; the dog's grip was a warning, no more. Used as she was to dogs, she was unafraid, but even so she froze. Which, if she'd thought about it, she realised she should have done as soon as she'd seen the dog making for her — rather than idiotically go forward the way she had.

Another sound caught her ears, though, and she looked up to see that help was at hand. But suddenly she was doubly shaken, and could only stare in astonishment at the tall, lean, aristocratic-looking man who had rounded that same corner in time to see all that had happened.

In stunned silence, her eyes huge, disbelieving, she stared at him. This man who, for the second time in two days, had come to her aid! But, as she recognised him from yesterday, so she knew that he had recognised her too.

It was all there in the way, in Czech, he called the dog off; as the dog immediately obeyed, let go of her and went to his master's side, the man, his charm of yesterday nowhere to be seen, blasted her in English with an angry, 'Haven't you *any* sense?'

Oh, no! Fabia mourned. Yesterday she had wanted to know the stranger's name. Today, she rather thought she knew it. Oh, lord, she inwardly groaned; if this was Vendelin Gajdusek, then she had a rather unhappy feeling that she had made a terrible start!

CHAPTER TWO

FABIA'S heart was beating hastily beneath her ribs as she observed from the dog lead in one of the man's hands that he either had just taken the animal for a walk or was just about to. The dog was now at 'sit' position by his master and was under strict control. But Fabia knew that there was no excuse for her foolhardiness.

She tried anyway, and began, 'I——' when she was abruptly cut off.

'Are you always so stupid!' the dark eyed man challenged angrily, his fuming glance going over her. 'Couldn't you see the dog didn't have friendship in mind when he hurled himself at you?'

'It wasn't like that!' she attempted to argue, but instantly saw that her remark hadn't gone down well. With some difficulty she swallowed down further argument, but was honest as she stated simply, 'It was my fault, not his. The dog was as good as telling me to stand still, but. . .'

'Show me your ankle,' the tall Czechoslovakian chopped her off.

'There's no. . .' She could have saved her breath, for, clearly not interested in her protest that there was no need, he intimated a place on a column by the door where she should put up her foot—and stood by, waiting none too patiently.

A further protest rose to her lips, but, since she had other more important matters to think about, she obligingly went and placed her foot on the ledge and, raising her trouser leg a little, allowed him to study her beige cotton sock where there was not so much as a broken thread.

'There's not a mark there,' she pulled back to comment as the tall man bent nearer.

'Take down your sock!' he instructed curtly.

'Oh, really!' she protested sharply, and received a withering look for her sins. 'All right, all right,' she quickly agreed as it dawned on her that if he *was* who she thought he was then she was going about it completely the wrong way if she hoped for an interview. Without further ado she busied herself in pulling her three-quarter-length beige cotton sock down from beneath her trouser leg, and down below her ankle.

To her astonishment, though, when the Dobermann had just held her in a gentle restraining grip, and no more than that, she could see that there were already small signs of bruising beginning to show on either side of her ankle.

The man's hand was warm, tinglingly warm, surprisingly gentle too on her skin, as he bent to examine her bruising and moved her foot this way and that. She heard him mutter something which might have been a mild swear word as he studied the Dobermann's handiwork, but, his examination over, she quickly pulled up her sock again, and just as quickly planted that foot alongside her other one.

He had straightened too when, anxious to get away from the wretched subject of his dog and her foolhardiness, she felt that it might be an idea if she stated her business. First, however, she decided to edge her way tactfully around the issue, and so began, 'You wouldn't happen to know if Miss Milada Pankracova has returned fr——'

'You're a friend of hers!' the man snarled before she could finish.

Grief—where was his charm of yesterday? Beginning to feel that she had imagined his charm, his inbuilt supply of it, Fabia strove hard to keep cool. 'I've never met her,' she replied quietly, and deciding that now was the time to come clean—albeit that she would be lying in her teeth, 'She, Miss Pankracova, arranged an interview for—er—me, with Mr Vendelin Gajdusek for last Friday, only he——'

A fiercer expletive than the one he had muttered before rent the air. Then the man was checking, and was remembering to speak in English. 'She did, did she?' he commented coldly. And sharply, 'Interview?' he questioned, and his eyes narrowing, 'Why would you want to interview him?' he challenged.

'I—work for *Verity* magazine,' Fabia lied to throw some light on it.

'You're a journalist!'

He knew darn well she, or rather Cara, was a journalist, Fabia thought crossly, all her vibes insisting that this man was the very same man she had come to interview. That being so, since it must have been he who had agreed to the interview with *Verity* magazine's representative to start with, he *must* know! But since to say as much might only set his back up, 'Yes,' she lied pleasantly, but felt not at all happy with the lie however pleasantly put, and went swiftly on, 'Er—do you—er— know Mr Gajdusek by any chance?'

'Better than most,' he confirmed, and Fabia's heart leapt excitedly. Here and now she was actually standing and talking with the great Vendelin Gajdusek! Some-how she rose over her excitement, though, and concen-trated all she could on the task at hand. Though before she could get in with a quick plea for an interview, Vendelin Gajdusek revealed that he had not for a moment forgotten the way in which the Dobermann had attached himself to her ankle, by decreeing, 'You'd better come into the house and have some antiseptic put on that wound.'

'Oh that's all right,' she answered blithely, adding

quite without thinking, 'In my job I often collect a scratch or two from some over-exuberant canine.' Oh, grief, she thought as she discovered his sharp glance on her — she was supposed to be a journalist, for goodness' sake! 'My parents, as well as having a smallholding, also run a boarding kennel,' she rapidly explained. 'I'm roped in to help whenever I visit them.' Hoping with all she had that that covered her blunder, she went on, less rapidly, 'My father is most insistent that my anti-tetanus jabs are kept up to date.'

To her immense relief, her explanation appeared to have been satisfactory. Vendelin Gajdusek did not question her, anyhow, though he still seemed to be insisting on the administration of some antiseptic, for, 'This way,' he instructed, and, turning, he gave an instruction to the Dobermann, who had not moved an inch since his last instruction. With the dog at heel beside him they walked round to the rear of the house.

Once through the rear door he issued another instruction to the animal, and as the animal sloped off — no doubt to some favourite spot in the house — the aggressive and now charmless man led the way to the kitchen.

'My housekeeper will know where the first-aid equipment is,' he clipped, and piloted her through a passage-way, and in through a solid wooden door. She recognised at once the well-built woman who turned from some chore at the kitchen sink as the woman who had opened the door to her last Friday. Fabia watched as, dropping the dog lead on to a large kitchen table, the dark man addressed a few remarks to the woman who then went to a drawer and took from it a large tin box and brought it to him. He took it from her and introduced his housekeeper, Mrs Edita Novakova, to her.

'How do you do?' Fabia murmured politely, for all she knew full well that the woman could not understand her.

But she received a warm smile from the housekeeper for her efforts, and as the housekeeper said something in Czech to her employer and, presumably with something to do elsewhere, left the kitchen, Vendelin Gajdusek turned his attention to Fabia. 'Take a seat here,' he instructed, pulling out a chair from the table. Then, while it seemed that he was the one who was going to apply the antiseptic — a job she could do quite well herself — he was speeding away any huffiness she felt at that last thought by asking her her name.

Fabia was ready for him this time, though, and had no intention of making another mistake, like the one she had made about her job. 'Cara Kingsdale,' she replied, and, while he ignored the fact that she had yesterday told him that her name was Fabia, she again experienced an uncomfortable feeling at having to lie to him.

To counteract that feeling, and while he propped her 'injured' foot on a stool and attended to her bruising, she opened her bag and extracted from it the envelope with Cara had handed over to her. As a matter of authenticity, and given that the appointment had been made two months ago and that perhaps Mr Gajdusek might need a little reminder, she took the letter from its envelope while, his touch again tingling, again gentle, he smoothed some cream over her bruises.

She had her sock neatly in place again, her foot off the stool, by the time he returned from the sink after washing the antiseptic off his hands. But he seemed taller than ever to her when, standing over her, he looked down into her large green eyes.

'Thank you, that was very good of you,' she murmured politely, but, feeling intimidated suddenly — or was that her guilty conscience again at work, she got to her feet and handed him the proof that she was who she said she was. 'You'll have a copy on file, of course,' she stated pleasantly, 'but. . .' Her voice tailed off as, opening out the letter, he began to read.

She saw him scowl darkly as he scanned the page, and wondered for a few moments if perhaps, although he could speak her tongue almost as if he'd been born in her country, he did not read English so well.

Any ideas on that score swiftly evaporated, however, when his glance suddenly shot to hers, and she was on the receiving end of his piercing eyes as, 'According to this, you should have been here last Friday!' he charged.

'I was,' she retorted, but swiftly realised that she was doing Cara no favours by snapping in retaliation, and bit back the 'but you weren't' which begged to be allowed to follow. Clearly the brute of a man had forgotten all about the interview—so too had Milada Pankracova, or she would have reminded him.

Had she been expecting any apology, though, Fabia realised then that she would have been disappointed for, 'Hrm,' was all he grunted, and, handing the letter back, he scrutinised her with a hard look, and Fabia had the feeling that he thought that *she* was the one in the wrong!

Starting to feel more than a fraction disgruntled that he'd been in Prague when she'd called before—on the right day *and* the right time—Fabia strove hard to keep what she was feeling out of her look. It wasn't fair, though, she silently railed. She'd been here on Friday, and he hadn't!

She was going on to recall how yesterday she had thought of Vendelin Gajdusek's being in Prague, when in actual fact, had she known it, he had been sitting right there beside her driving her back to Mariánské Lázně, when he suddenly gave her near heart failure by challenging, out of the blue 'I thought you said your name was Fabia?'

'I did,' she replied, there being nothing else she could

reply. 'It's a name my family call me,' she excused. 'A name my friends use, too.'

'Do I thank you that yesterday you thought me a friend?' he questioned drily, and for a moment she thought she caught a glimpse of yesterday's charm in his look.

'Yesterday you were a very Good Samaritan,' she smiled, and took the opportunity, while he seemed halfway friendly, to enquire, 'I don't suppose it would be convenient for me to interview you now, Mr Gajdusek, would it?'

For a brief while he looked down at her from his superior height. Then, even while she was desperately trying to remember a quarter of the questions she was supposed to ask him, 'No,' he replied succinctly, 'it would not.' And, while her hopes dropped down to basement level, 'Now,' he added, 'I'm taking Azor for his walk.'

'Oh,' Fabia mumbled, feeling crestfallen. But with energy to spare she would dearly have liked to go with him and his dog Azor for a good long walk. Again, though, there were some things which she was not well enough acquainted with him to mention—especially now that she knew who her Good Samaritan of yesterday was. So, hoisting her bag over her shoulder with an element of pride that for a brief moment made her lose sight of how important it was to try and pin him down for an interview, she made for the door.

His voice stopped her before she reached it, however, and a smile crazily beamed its way up from her toes when, 'Want to walk with me?' he drawled.

The smile was in her eyes, on her lips as, charmed again, she spun round, 'Can I?' she accepted eagerly.

His eyes rested on her beautifully shaped mouth, then went up to her eyes and held her look steadily before he flicked his glance down to her sensible shoes. Fabia gathered that he approved of her walking shoes, but, even so, it did not stop him from warning, some-what severely, I'm not turning back in five minutes.'

'Good!' she promptly responded. 'Some of the dogs at home — my parents' home when I'm there,' she tacked on hastily, 'have to be walked miles.'

Vendelin Gajdusek flicked one last look at her, leaving her with no idea whether he approved or disapproved, and, pausing only to pick up the dog's lead, he went to the kitchen door with her.

As Fabia had suspected, the dog Azor did not take long to find. Indeed, it would appear that the Dober-mann's sense of hearing was so acute that, even with the kitchen door closed, he could hear the rattle of his dog lead. For, as his master opened the kitchen door, there, in eager anticipation, stood Azor.

They left the house by the same route by which they had entered, though had not gone far when her escort stopped to exchange a few words with an odd-job man who was undertaking a minor repair near some outbuildings.

Fabia opted to saunter on to keep her eye on Azor who, as yet still unleashed, had decided to trot around sniffing as he went.

'That was Ivo, my housekeeper's husband,' Vendelin Gajdusek enlightened her as he fell into step with her and she sharpened up her pace, to match his.

'Ah — Mr Novakova,' Fabia pronounced, privately of the view that the name Ivo Novakova was one to get the jaws working.

She rather suspected that Vendelin Gajdusek thought so too when a swift glance to his face showed a hint of a smile was playing around his mouth. She discovered though that it was not the odd-job man's name which was causing him mild amusement, but her! For, 'Mr Novak,' he corrected, adding, 'in a majority of Czech names, "ova" is added to the end of a man's surname for his wife when he marries.'

'I'll have to remember that,' Fabia commented cheerfully, and, oddly, felt no end uplifted when Vendelin Gajdusek's smile did make it.

After that the walk progressed splendidly as far as she was concerned. She enjoyed being out in the crisp fresh air, enjoyed every moment of stepping out on well-worn pathways with trees all around.

A mile or so on, however, and thoughts of Cara began bouncing in and out of her head. She couldn't help thinking that Cara, who had been known to take the car to go as far as the corner shop to pick up a bottle of milk, would have folded long before this. Perhaps it was as well that it was she and not her sister who was here, she thought at one point — and then immediately realised how ridiculous that thought was. Apart from the fact that Cara would professionally streamline her way through any interview she effected with Mr Gajdusek, Cara would never have worn 'sensible' shoes to start with. So the question of her taking a five-mile hike across what in parts was sometimes rough terrain would never have occurred.

What did occur to Fabia just then was that, given that *she* was supposed to be the journalist, she was making a dreadful mess of it. She had already experienced difficulty in pinning her fellow walker down to an interview and, for all she could tell, might have further difficulty in that area. So what, for goodness' sake, was she doing letting this heaven-sent chance slip by without asking a few pertinent questions?

'Do you take Azor for a long walk every day, Mr Gajdusek?' she asked for innocent openers.

'You obviously enjoy walking,' he countered, and looked over to her, to where a hint of lovely colour now showed in her normally pale porcelain-like skin. A moment later their glances met and, disturbingly, Fabia suddenly experienced a moment of confusion, and forgot for a while that he had not answered her — question.

'I grew up in the country,' she murmured, not sure why she had told him that because it had no bearing on the subject. Cara had grown up in the country too of course, but wouldn't walk anywhere if she could avoid it.

'Where in England?' he asked.

'Gloucestershire,' she saw no harm in telling him, and realised then that she had again forgotten her quest — that interview. 'Tell me, Mr Gajdusek,' she began as they strode out from woodland and into a sun drenched clearing, 'do — ?'

'It's too beautiful a day for you to go on Mr Gajduseking me the whole while,' he cut her off in easy fashion.

Her breath caught, and she sent him a startled look and, as her heart gave a merry flutter to see that his dark-eyed glance, dark *and* good-humoured if she was not mistaken, was on her again, 'Are you inviting me to call you — Vendelin?' she dared, and hardly believed that it could be so.

But looking at him still, she saw the corners of his mouth pick up slightly, and suddenly, so were the corners of *her* mouth, because, 'My friends call me Ven,' he advised her, and solemnly added, 'Fabia.'

And it was then that she laughed, then that after so much recent trauma her world suddenly righted itself and she felt happy again. The man she was here to interview had suggested she call him Ven, had even, if jokingly, suggested that they might be friends. Her worries and cares oddly seemed to just desert her.

Fabia soon realised that her euphoria of the moment could not last, of course. For one thing, she was still here to do that job for her sister. For another, there was still Barney to worry about. Not to mention her car. Now how could she have forgotten her car! She. . .

Her thoughts broke off when she found that Vendelin Gajdusek's glance was still on her—as though he had enjoyed the sound of her light laugh. Abruptly she looked in another direction—somehow, she felt unsteady, as if everything was getting away from her!

It was then, when it came to her that Vendelin Gajdusek was heady stuff, that she took herself severely to task. Some seconds later she was discounting that he had anything whatsoever to do with any of her peculiar thoughts and emotions. For heaven's sake, she'd been under a bit of strain of late, so what was more natural than that, having at last met the man she had been at pains to meet—actually being out walking with him, and on such a lovely sharp but sunny day—she should—er—relax a little?

'Mr Gajdusek. . .' she promptly decided to get in with another of her interview questions, though she made the mistake of looking at him, and his raised-eyebrow glance at her stopped her. 'Er—V-Ven. . .' She faltered.

'Tell me, Fabia,' he cut in smoothly, 'are there any more at home like you?'

'I'm sorry?' she queried, not quite sure what he was asking.

'You're twenty-two, I think you said,' he reminded her when she would rather that he hadn't. Heartily wishing she had never been provoked into volunteering that piece of information, Fabia didn't want him getting the idea that at twenty-two she couldn't be a too well-seasoned journalist. But his comment on her age was a throwaway one, it seemed, for he followed it up with a reference to his previous question by asking, 'Are you an only child?'

She was grateful to be away from the subject of her age and told him honestly, 'I've an elder sister,' and, on thinking briefly, added, 'but she's in America at the moment.' Swiftly, she went to change the subject — but he beat her to it.

'I expect you do quite a bit of travelling in your work?' he probed, when she wanted to be the one asking the questions.

'I should like to travel more,' she answered diplomatically, and getting in quickly, 'How about you? Do you do much travelling?'

Her question never got answered, for just then another couple with a dog appeared in the distance and Vendelin Gajdusek was calling Azor to heel so that he could leash him. 'We'll return to the house this way,' he then informed Fabia, and guided her in a different direction.

They had walked quite some miles, she realised on the return journey, and she had been in his company for quite some while, so it came as no surprise to also realise how totally unsuited she was for the job she was there to do. Any journalist worth her salt would have got scads more out of the tall Czechoslovakian than she had, she thought glumly.

A few seconds later however, and she was wondering, Would they, though? So far as she could make out, Ven Gajdusek was more interested in enjoying his walk than he was in answering any of her questions.

On that thought, a streak of fairness smote Fabia and she became guiltily aware that, since he must spend a good deal of his time cooped up in his office, it was no wonder that he wanted to enjoy his walks without any prying journalist asking the 'whys and wherefores' of everything.

Of course, he had *agreed* to the interview, she counter-argued. Yes, but not particularly when he was resting from his labours. Oh, blow it, she thought a little crossly, and, getting absolutely nowhere with her argument, she resolved that she would ask him not one interview-type question for the remainder of the walk

but that, once back at the house, she would ask him to
honour his promise regarding that interview.

With that settled, they were back by the outbuildings
near the house when she again remembered her car and
thought she had better find out where it was garaged
before she again forgot to bring it up. 'By the way,' she
began, hardly able to credit that, when earlier that
morning her car had been such a concern to her, great
expanses of time should now elapse without her giving
it so much as a thought, 'could you tell me the name of
the garage where my car——'

She was getting a little fed up with the habit he had
of never allowing her to finish a sentence. He did it
again. 'Why?' he cut in.

'Why?' she returned thunderstruck. 'Why, to telephone and ask how——'

'My apologies,' he cut in evenly, 'I hadn't realised
that you spoke my language.'

'I don't,' she told him, a shade edgily it was true, but
then, for all he understood, and spoke *her* language,
she still didn't have a clue what he was talking about.

'Then how do you propose to make your enquiry?'
he threw some daylight into her fog.

'They don't speak English at the garage?'

'I'm afraid not,' he replied, and might have added
more, but just then a car, a Skoda, driven by a man of
about thirty, came slowly around to the rear of the
house, and parked on a car standing area.

They were close up to the car when the brown-haired
man of average build left his car and Ven Gajdusek
halted to exchange a few words in Czech with him.
Then, his manners in company nothing if not impec-
cable, Ven switched to English and introduced Lubor
Ondrus.

'Lubor, Miss Kingsdale, a visitor from England,' he
finished the introduction.

'Ah, Miss Cara Kingsdale,' Lubor beamed, shaking hands while looking at her admiringly.

'You know of Miss Kingsdale?' Ven questioned him sharply.

'Only from the business card I found on my desk,' the other replied, his English excellent. 'I asked Edita about it; she said she had put it there.'

'I called last Friday,' Fabia mentioned, rescuing her hand from Lubor Ondrus, who appeared to enjoy holding on to it. Since his desk must be in the house, perhaps he was Ven Gajdusek's research assistant, she mused, and Edita had mistakenly placed the card on his desk instead of Milada Pankracova's.

'I'm so sad that I missed you,' Lubor Ondrus said soulfully, explaining, 'I returned only last evening from a few days' holiday.' And while Fabia was comprehending that here was a flirt of the first water, he was asking, 'But perhaps, despite your business card, you are on holiday in my country.'

'I'm hoping to see something of Czechoslovakia while I'm here,' she replied, but as it suddenly struck her that the silence emanating from Ven Gajdusek was decidedly chilly—and since the last thing she needed was to be bad friends with him if he objected to Lubor Ondrus flirting with her on his time, 'But now I must return to my hotel,' she added.

'Perhaps I may be permitted to take you,' Lubor jumped in before she could draw another breath.

She was spared having to find a tactful reply, however, when his employer immediately, and unceremoniously, thrust the dog lead at him and instructed, 'You can take Azor, I have to go out—I'll drive Miss Kingsdale to her hotel.'

Fabia looked from one to the other and wanted to be a duty to neither. 'I can walk,' she began, and might have added that she would have enjoyed to do that—had she got the chance.

But, 'You have walked enough!' Ven Gajdusek informed her, exceedingly autocratically in her opinion. Though when she might have let him know that she was quite able to make her own decisions, thank you very much, she remembered — she still wanted that interview with him. 'This way,' he stated, and, barely giving her time to make her goodbyes to Lubor Ondrus, he was guiding her over to where his car was garaged.

Not for a moment had she thought that she would ever be given a lift in the Mercedes again. But as she sat beside Ven Gajdusek while the car rolled silently downhill and into Mariánské Lázně, and she recovered her normally even temper, she couldn't have said that she was too put out by the experience.

They were nearly into the spa town, and were waiting while a trolley-bus took right of way, when she saw no reason not to ask what seemed to her a perfectly natural question. 'Is Lubor Ondrus your research assistant?' she enquired politely — and promptly wished she hadn't.

For, 'No!' he replied shortly, and gave his attention over to his driving.

'Oh,' she said flatly.

Then felt a mixture of relief and confusion when, relenting from that monosyllabic answer, he deigned to enlighten her, 'He's my secretary.'

'Oh,' she mumbled again, and just had to ask then what didn't really need asking, but more — confirming, 'So you have two secretaries?'

But 'No,' he repeated, just that, and left her to work the rest of it out.

'Are you saying that Miss Pankracova no longer works for you?' Fabia asked in some startlement when, after some seconds of sifting through that last 'No', that was all she could come up with.

'I was pleased to let her go!' he replied, and Fabia didn't like the sound of that one little bit.

'You gave her the sack?' she questioned quickly.

'Sack?' he enquired, as if the word in the context she used it was unknown to him.

'Fired — dismissed,' she offered a couple of alternatives — only to find that he found her first offering of more interest.

'Sack,' he played with the word, and asked, 'Where, in the context of dismissal, did it originate?'

'I don't *know*!' she exclaimed exasperatedly, anxiety suddenly getting to her as she all at once recognised that they were nearly at her hotel — and she had nothing fixed about the interview yet! Though, on looking across at him, and observing that one eyebrow had ascended aloft at what he must consider was the sharpness of her answer, she realised that she was never likely to get an interview if she did not control her exasperation at his evasive non-answers to most of her questions. Swiftly, she swallowed her ire and, taking a steadying breath, 'Well,' she began, 'so far as I know — and I could be wrong — I believe it has something to do with years back when a tradesman was dismissed, he would pack his tools in the sack he carried them in, and walk off the job.' And, with that out of the way, unless Ven Gajdusek wanted more — and she wouldn't put that past him — she just had to ask, 'Milada Pankracova's leaving your employ won't affect anything, will it?'

'Affect?' he threw back at her — most infuriatingly as far as she was concerned because she was positive that he knew full well this time the context in which she used the word.

But, as he drew the car up outside her hotel and turned to look at her, Fabia knew that she couldn't afford to be infuriated. Soon he would go — this last minute had to count. 'May I still have the interview with you which you promised?' she asked straight out — and thought for a few seconds, as he looked sternly at her, that she had blown it, and that he had taken the

strongest exception to her reminding him of his
promise.

His expression stayed stern and Fabia, trying to read
his thoughts, started to squirm inwardly. She felt certain
then that he must be thinking that if she was any sort of
a journalist that she could do quite a write-up out of
the considerable time she had just spent walking in his
sole company. Either that, or perhaps that she hadn't
asked very many pointed questions. How could she,
though, when in all politeness. . .? Perhaps that was
the trouble — perhaps she was being too polite. Not that
she could see anyone getting this man to answer any
questions if he decided against it.

As was proved when, without replying to her question about the interview, he left the driver's seat and
came round to the passenger's door. With the awful
feeling in her bones that she really *had* blown it, Fabia
got out of the car and stood with him on the pavement.

But, as she looked up into his dark eyes that gave
nothing away, and battled furiously against the pride
that would have held her back from pressing her
question, suddenly the sun came out. For, even as he
started to walk away from her, he drawled, 'You'd
better dine with me tomorrow.'

This was no time for false modesty. 'What time?'
burst from her rapidly as he reached the driver's door.

She saw the corners of his mouth try to twitch up as
if her snatching at his invitation had amused him. But
his smile was severely repressed as he replied, 'I'll send
Ivo for you about seven.'

Fabia, not wanting him to think that she hung on his
every word, turned away. She was walking into the hotel
when she heard his car start up. She carried on walking.

Strangely, though, as a smile lit her face, she couldn't
in all honesty have said that her smile was *totally* on
account of having secured an interview with that most
elusive man!

CHAPTER THREE

HAVING slept better that night, Fabia awakened on Tuesday and thought of Ven, thought of Cara and of Barney, and would dearly have liked to telephone her parents to find out if they had heard anything from her sister. But, since Cara was supposed to be with her in Czechoslovakia and had said that she'd be doing her a favour if she didn't ring them, Fabia settled for the next best thing. Some time after breakfast she went and bought a picture postcard to send home. Then, strolling past Mariánské Lázně's colonnade, she walked on and into an area of well-kept parkland and, taking her ease on one of the white-painted benches scattered around, found the card and began to write.

Ten minutes afterwards she had filled every available space on the card with news of her journey and her impressions of beautiful Mariánské Lázně, so that when it came to penning a signature there was barely any room for her own name, let alone room to add Cara's.

Leaving her bench, Fabia next took another stroll around the town which so enchanted her. She walked along some residential streets, and once observed with some fascination that a coal delivery had been deposited outside one house, and that the coal was brown! Having never seen brown coal before, she presumed the house owner would shovel the load down to his cellar when convenient. She stored that memory away, together with the memory of the forest in the foreground as she walked on.

Soon she came by the local gymnasium, and then the local Cedok tourist office, and from there she turned into a part which she was growing more familiar with, and in no time found she was back in the colonnade area.

By then it was getting on for lunchtime but, sauntering through the colonnade, she couldn't resist first climbing a flight of stairs to take a look at some of the splendid Bohemian glassware on display.

Twenty minutes later, carrying a carefully packaged beautiful glass vase which she knew her parents—well, her mother in particular—were just going to love, Fabia came down the stairs again and, stepping out into the colonnade, bumped right into none other than Lubor Ondrus.

'Hello!' he greeted her at once, clearly delighted to have met her.

'Hello,' she returned, and discovered that it was quite pleasant to bump into someone she knew.

'You have been shopping?' he beamed, flicking his glance to the parcel she held.

'A present for my parents,' she replied.

'You must be exhausted,' he immediately suggested, when she was nothing of the kind. But, never one to miss an opportunity, 'I insist that you allow me to take you to lunch,' he followed up, and smilingly waited.

What should she do? Fabia wondered. He was transparent, but nice. A flirt, but open with it. He was friendly too, and she rather thought she liked him. 'I can show you an excellent view of the town,' he pressed, his smile dipping for all the world as if he would take it as a personal tragedy if she refused.

'Er—thank you very much,' she accepted, and had to smile herself when his beaming smile instantly burst into life.

'My car is not far away,' he informed her, taking charge of her parcel, and carrying it to where his car was parked.

'This place we're going to, it's in Mariánské Lázně?'

she thought she should enquire, since it seemed they would not be walking to this lunchtime venue.

'But yes,' he replied as he attentively opened the passenger door of his Skoda for her. 'I have correspondence to deal with this afternoon and must return to my work.'

Fabia got into the vehicle and wondered for some moments about his employer. He had taken some time off yesterday morning to take Azor, and incidentally her, for a long walk. Did Ven Gajdusek work only afternoons? Or perhaps afternoons and evenings? Or maybe to take the morning off to exercise his dog was a rarity?

Only then did she realise that, for all she had been in his company for a total of several hours now, she still didn't know the first thing about him. In fact, she knew little more about him now than before she had met him — Cara would make mincemeat of her if she knew that!

Feeling unable to see just then how Cara, even with her journalistic experience, would have fared better with a man who, somehow without you noticing, turned every question or countered it with one of his own, Fabia resolved, as Lubor Ondrus turned into a driveway and steered the Skoda uphill, to do better.

'We will eat first,' Lubor smiled, parking his car and escorting her into a smart hotel.

Bearing in mind that she would be eating a main meal that evening, Fabia ordered an omelette and salad, and soon discovered that once Lubor had settled down from his initial opportunistic manner he was quite a pleasant lunchtime companion.

'Is it permitted for me to call you Cara?' he enquired, having just asked that she use his first name.

'Of course,' she replied, 'but. . .' She broke off. She wasn't happy being Cara, wasn't comfortable with the name; it wasn't hers.

'I am being too — too. . .forward?' Lubor questioned, soon putting a smile back on her face that, when he ranked as far from backward among her list of acquaintances, he should have to *ask* if he was being forward!

'No, it isn't that,' she quickly soothed his fears, real or assumed. And, while her guilty conscience took another stab, 'Actually, most people use the name my family call me — Fabia,' she told him.

'Fabia,' he repeated, seeming to enjoy the way it rolled around his tongue. And, quickly taking her name on board, 'You are here in Czechoslovakia on business and holiday, Fabia, I think?'

'Yes,' she agreed, though while she felt it would not be right for her to question him about his employer, she could see no reason — since he must be aware of the contents of Ven Gajdusek's desk diary — for not mentioning, 'I came here specifically to interview Mr Gajdusek last Friday, but——'

'Mr Gajdusek has agreed to an interview!' Lubor exclaimed in some surprise.

'Yes,' she answered, a little surprised herself by Lubor's attitude. 'Didn't you know?' she asked.

'I have no note of it — and he *never* gives interviews,' her lunchtime companion stated categorically.

'I know. My s. . .' She broke off, caught unawares having been about to reveal that her sister had told her. 'Which is why it's so super that he agreed to this interview,' she quickly covered her slip.

'He definitely agreed to this?' Lubor still seemed to her to be unsure.

'Didn't Milada Pankracova leave you a note?' Fabia asked, beginning to wish she had never said anything. Clearly the previous secretary had not been a very efficient worker — perhaps that was why Ven had dismissed her.

'No, but. . .' He broke off, appeared thoughtful and then, suddenly, as light seemed to dawn, he was back

to his own smiling self. 'I had wondered why Mr
Gajdusek had me checking through Milada Pankracov-
a's — um — past work yesterday. Now, I think I know.'

'Er — she's made some mistakes?' Fabia questioned.

'More than most, I would say,' he smiled. 'But now
let us talk about you.'

'But — my interview for last Friday,' Fabia questioned
on a sudden dart of panic, 'it was recorded in Mr
Gajdusek's diary?'

'Of course — but unfortunately overlooked,' he
replied straight away, and as it came to her that he
must have been teasing her with his earlier attitude, he
was asking, 'Now, can I get you a glass of wine?'

'Only a small one,' she accepted and, her dart of
panic gone, felt a return of her reluctance to ask
probing questions about his work, and more particularly about his employer, so gave herself over to enjoying this lunchtime interlude.

She did enjoy it, too. Though when the meal was
ended and they went outside it was to discover that it
had begun to drizzle. 'I am afraid the view will not now
be as good as I promised,' Lubor apologised. 'But we
will go and look just the same,' he decided, and, taking
her by the arm, he guided her to the front of the
building and over to a high parapet. 'We should have
looked first!' he declared abjectly when all they could
see of the scene below and beyond was of rooftops and
forest shrouded in mist and rain. 'Perhaps we can come
again tomorrow?' he turned to suggest eagerly, while at
the same time he took the opportunity to place one arm
familiarly about her shoulders.

'I'm not sure what I'll be doing tomorrow,' Fabia
declined. She liked him still but felt that the familiarity
of his uninvited arm about her shoulder called for
backing-away tactics.

If she had thought she was showing him a stop-light,
however, *he* must have seen it as a green one, for his

arm suddenly tightened and there was a definite amorous gleam in his eye as he edged closer to her and
breathed seductively, 'I like you *so* much, Fabia.'

In any other circumstances, Fabia felt that she might
have been a trace worried—it wasn't every day that she
was in a foreign land, with a foreign male who, having
fed her, tried his hand at seducing her. But nor was it
every day that in broad daylight—given that the light
wasn't all that good—that she stood in what was now
quite heavy rain getting soaked while her amorous
swain waited for her to make the next move.

She rather thought he was hoping for some reciprocal
comment or gesture, but for the life of her, whether he
thought it unforgivable or not, she just had to burst out
laughing, and 'Lubor!' she laughed. 'I'm getting wet!'

At once he was contrite, and in seconds he was
hurrying her to his car. Once they were inside, he
steered it downhill. At the bottom, where the hotel
drive met the highway, he halted and was watching the
traffic on his left when Fabia, traces of amusement still
on her face, looked to the right and suddenly felt all
amusement vanish. For there, heading towards them,
indeed about to go by, was a Mercedes, its driver being
Ven Gajdusek! A Ven Gajdusek, she swiftly realised,
who had recognised not only the Skoda but its occu-
pants too, and, from the look of fury on his face, was
not very pleased to see any of them.

Oh, heavens, she thought, and tried to discount a
dreadful feeling that it wasn't his secretary so much that
he was furious to see, but her! Though before she could
speculate on that point, Lubor, entirely unaware that
his employer had passed them, was turning to state,
'You are even more beautiful with your face washed
with rain.'

A minute or so earlier she might have burst out
laughing again at what she considered was an 'over the
top' compliment but—and she owned that seeing Ven

Gajdusek was to blame — she suddenly felt in a laughing mood no longer.

So 'Thank you, Lubor,' she accepted quietly, and received another of his beaming smiles before, the way clear, he moved off into traffic.

It took only minutes for Lubor to drive her to her hotel, but as she thanked him for lunch and he handed her back her parcel, he replied, 'Lunch was a happy time for me also,' and didn't waste a moment to enquire, 'Shall we have a happy dinner together this evening?'

'I'm afraid not,' she replied, finding a regretful smile, for she was certain he was quite harmless. 'I have a business engagement,' she excused, and wondered for a moment if Lubor had guessed that her business engagement for that evening was with his employer, or if perhaps he already knew from some office discussion with him that she was dining with Ven? She immediately discounted that idea, realising that, had Lubor known, then he obviously wouldn't have asked her to dine himself.

She said goodbye to him but by the time she had entered the hotel, Lubor was already far from her thoughts. Memory of Ven Gajdusek's furious expression of a short while ago returned, and as she waited for her room key she began to grow seriously worried.

Fabia went up to her room unable to find any reason why he should have looked so furious. Though for one quite dreadful moment she wondered if, English not being his first language, he had meant that he would *lunch* with her that day, and not *dine*. That would explain his fury — anyone would be furious in the circumstance of witnessing her leaving a hotel at lunchtime with someone else.

A moment later, though, and Fabia was scrapping that theory, for she had just remembered how Ven had parted from her with the words, 'I'll send Ivo for you about seven.' Seven was lunchtime in nobody's book!

Why the fury, then? she fretted, and then started to have terrible gnawing doubts about whether or not she was truly dining with him that night. Was it the case that he had not *told* Lubor he was having a business dinner with her that evening purely and simply because he did not *consider* that he had a dinner engagement with her?

But yesterday he'd specifically stated, 'You'd better dine with me tomorrow,' and he wouldn't go back on his word, would he? She felt bad enough as it was, so it just wasn't the moment to remember how he'd 'overlooked' having agreed to see her last Friday!

When her inner disquiet began to peak in case Ven Gajdusek might once again 'overlook' that he had agreed to see her, Fabia got out of her damp clothes and went to wash her hair and take a bath.

Feeling restless once her hair was dried, she donned a shirt and a pair of trousers and nipped down to the foyer to post the card she had written to her parents. '*Děkuji*,' she tried out a Czech thank-you to the man on Reception who sold her a stamp for three crowns and assured her her card would catch that day's post.

But the small errand took up barely any time and she returned to her room with some hours to go before she would know if Ven Gajdusek was going to honour his letter. Conscience gave her an uncomfortable nip, for it couldn't exactly be said to be the height of honour for her to accept his invitation to dine in his home in the guise of a journalist when she wasn't one, but Fabia went and studied her wardrobe.

At ten to seven she had been ready for twenty minutes. At five to seven she decided that her long gold hair needed another combing—and jumped up from the dressing-table as if shot when a minute later the phone in her room rang and the receptionist told her that a car had come for her.

'Thank you,' she replied, too stewed-up suddenly to remember the Czechoslovakian word for it.

Once she had put the phone down, however, Fabia took a moment or two out to compose herself. She owned that her insides were in a mammoth flutter, but there were several reasons for that. For one thing, she had by then been convinced that she could forget Ven Gajdusek's 'I'll send Ivo for you. . .'. Yet here was Ivo come for her. For another—here was she with no experience whatsoever of professional interviewing techniques—not even a rank amateur, in fact—yet she was about to pretend that interviewing was second nature to her.

It was of no help to her inner disquiet, as she left her room, that she saw in her mind's eye a picture of the aristocratic-looking Ven Gajdusek. Oh, heavens, she panicked, and knew then that her impersonation would have to be good—Ven Gajdusek was nobody's fool.

How she managed to find a smile for Ivo when she saw him waiting for her in the foyer, she didn't know. But smile she did, and even managed to find a Czechoslovakian good evening, as 'Dobrý večer,' she greeted him.

She still felt full of inner disquiet as the car zigzagged out of town and started to wind its way up to her host's home. It had heartened her though that, probably from basic good manners, she had been able to mask her reluctance to get into the car with Ivo, and had even found a smile for him. She would have similarly to hide from his employer the fact that she felt a wreck inside. Ivo drew the car up at the front door, she pinned her hopes, rather desperately, she owned, on one very big, important fact. That fact that, since Vendelin Gajdusek had apparently never been interviewed by any journalist, he would not see anything out of the ordinary in her particular interviewing technique.

'*Děkuji mnohokrát*,' she thanked Ivo very much when he escorted her to the door of his master's home. And, '*Dobrý večer, Paní Novakova*,' she greeted the housekeeper with a smile when almost at once the door was opened.

'*Dobrý večer, Slečno Kingsdale*,' the housekeeper replied with a smile of her own—but a movement to the right of them caused Fabia, a smile still on her mouth, to turn and see an immaculately suited Ven Gajdusek.

'Good evening, Fabia,' he greeted her smoothly as the housekeeper melted away, his dark eyes flicking over her from the top of her golden head, taking in her features and perfect complexion before travelling over her long-sleeved fine wool lime-coloured dress, its straight lines hiding none of her femininity, before his all-assessing gaze ended at her neat two-and-a-half-inch-heel shoes.

'Good evening, Mr G. . .' she began to reply, but his glance was already away from her shoes, and he was giving her a slightly raised eyebrow look. '. . .Er—Ven,' she completed—and saw a hint of a smile touch his quite devastating-looking mouth, before he touched a hand to her elbow, and guided her to his drawing-room.

It was a tasteful room. A gracious room. A room of high ceilings, good-quality furnishings, with a well-polished antique occasional table here and there. 'Take a seat while I get you something to drink,' he invited, indicating what looked like the last word in comfort in the shape of a couch—one of a pair in the room. 'What will you have?' he enquired, going over to a drinks table while she tested out the couch and discovered that its appearance of comfort was no lie.

'A gin and tonic, please,' she replied, and, when he

brought it over and set it down before her on a low table, 'It's very good of you to see me,' she thought she should mention.

'My pleasure,' he murmured suavely, and from then until Mrs Novakova came in to tell them that dinner was ready he engaged her in surface conversation that had nothing whatsoever to do with the reason for why she was there.

Taking her cue from him, Fabia realised then that perhaps barely to step over his threshold and then at once to launch into the dozens of questions she must ask him was perhaps, in this gracious room, rather graceless. So she held back on her questioning, though she somehow found that she was telling him of her love of music and how Janáček's lively sixth movement was one of her particular favourites.

Indeed, Fabia was still wondering how the deuce he had got her talking about music when they transferred to an equally gracious and charming dining-room. She still hadn't found an answer when the housekeeper came in and served the first course. *Plněná sardelová vejce* was a tasty concoction of egg and anchovy, and Fabia gave her attention over to other matters.

'This is quite delicious,' she remarked to her host, and when he looked over at her quite affably, with no sign of the fury that had enveloped him at lunchtime, she felt that she could, and should, bring the matter into the open. And did so, with a smiling, 'It makes me very glad I only ate a light lunch today.'

His look on her was steady, cool. 'You lunched with my secretary, I believe,' he returned evenly.

'I bumped into him while I was out,' she explained. 'It was kind of him to invite me. He's a very friendly person,' she thought to add.

'Have you looked at yourself in the mirror lately?' Ven commented drily. Fabia felt the most unexpected warm glow inside that surely there had to be a compli-

ment in there somewhere? That glow was swiftly damp-
ened, however, as she realised that in one and the same
breath he was as good as saying that he was aware of
Lubor Ondrus's propensity to flirt with any female who
was a quarter way pretty.

'He didn't try to flirt with me the whole time,' she
defended, and half wished then that she hadn't said
anything about lunchtime. 'We talked a lot,' she went
on. 'He told me that there was a wonderful view, but it
came on to rain and——'

'What else did he tell you?' Abruptly, and with a
habit she had been on the way to forgetting he had,
Ven Gajdusek cut her off again.

Startled by his sharp tone, Fabia stared at him in
some surprise. But, as she all at once realised that he
thought, actually thought, that she had been pumping
his secretary about him, so a tide of pink warmed her
cheeks, and, 'Nothing!' she exclaimed hotly, more
startlement hitting her as it dawned on her that this
then was the reason for his fury when he'd seen them
together. 'Good heavens,' she flew, feeling outraged
that he could suspect her of such a thing, 'I wouldn't
dream of asking him questions about you!'

'You wouldn't?' he queried coolly, his eyes on the
angry sparks flashing in hers.

'Of course not,' she replied in no uncertain terms,
and though still angry, as his eyes stayed steady and
speculative on hers, she would dearly have loved to
have known what he was thinking.

Any chance to pursue her line of thought, however,
was lost just then when the housekeeper came in to
clear away their first course, and, with Ven exchanging
a word or two with her, serve the second course.

Fabia ate a morsel of a tasty mushroom-filled pork
cutlet that had a hint of caraway in there somewhere
and, more in an attempt to recapture some of her

former equilibrium than anything, she asked, 'Has this dish any special name?'

'I thought you might wish to know, which is why I enquired of Edita,' he replied urbanely, 'But I'm afraid it is nothing more than plain *"vepřové řízky plněné žampióny"*.'

Plain or not, Fabia reckoned it would take her a fortnight to learn to say it. But, unblinking, she stared at him, 'And the wine?' she enquired of the rather delicious chilled white wine that went with it.

'*Rülander*, a product of Moravia,' he informed her, and asked, 'It pleases your palate?'

'Very much,' she replied, but she somehow still felt upset that he could think she would go behind his back and cross-examine his secretary. It niggled away at her for about perhaps another two seconds, then, apropos of nothing, almost without her own volition, she found that she was suddenly bursting out, 'The only time your name was mentioned at lunchtime was when I stated that I was here, in Czechoslovakia, to interview you.'

'I'm not sure whether I should be flattered or otherwise,' her host drawled, and she decided on the spot that she hated men with sophisticated wit—was he saying that he took it as a compliment, or not, that he only got one mention at lunchtime?

'Anyhow,' she resumed, having no time then to fathom it, 'at first Lubor Ondrus, only out of devilment I'm sure, seemed surprised that you'd agreed to an interview. Then, suddenly, he relented and told me that my proposed interview with you was recorded in your desk diary, but that it had been overlooked.' There, she felt better for having got that off her chest. Though the dark-eyed man opposite was wearing that inscrutable look again, and once more she discovered that she would dearly like to know what he was thinking.

But, 'Lubor Ondrus is a first-class secretary,' was his only comment. And, setting warning bells off in her head, 'And you, Fabia, are, I'm sure, a first-class journalist.' Oh, grief, she thought and suspected that now was the time she must get in with her interview questions. 'Have you been doing it long?' he enquired.

Oh, help, she thought, wishing with all she had that she'd never told him that she was twenty-two. 'Er — since I left school,' she replied, and felt hot all over in case he wanted a run-down on her work experience in the world of journalism.

'Do you use shorthand?'

Shouldn't she be asking that question? 'My own kind,' she replied, and getting ready to put a few questions from her list, she paused to smile — and found that he could find his questions faster.

'You type, of course?' he queried conversationally, and suddenly Fabia felt panic hit the pit of her stomach. If he offered her the use of one of his typewriters, she was done for.

Somehow, though, she managed to keep her head, 'Of course,' she replied, but quickly followed up, 'Though I always prefer to write my work down in longhand first.'

Fabia was still wondering if she needed to add anything to that when, as a complete switch, and taking her totally off guard, Ven threw the abrupt question, 'Are you married?'

'No,' she answered at once — and immediately realised her mistake. She was supposed to be Cara, and Cara *was* married. She should have said yes. Too late now, though Cara would murder her if she messed this up. On thinking about it, however, since Cara still used her maiden name professionally, she didn't see how that little slip would matter all that much. She pushed her mistake to the back of her mind — and then found that, although the question was on her list, that she was asking off her own bat, and with no thought to that list, 'Are *you* married?'

He shook his head. 'Never tempted,' he replied, and while Fabia recognised that there would be a good few women sorry about that, 'Boyfriends?' he queried.

'No one special,' she replied lightly.

'Which is perhaps why you can come to Czechoslovakia for a holiday alone, a working holiday,' he qualified with some charm. And, while she was suddenly a little mesmerised to see a return of that charm, 'You mentioned to my secretary yesterday that you were hoping to see something of my country,' he reminded her. 'Do you have any part in mind?'

'Well, Prague, of course,' she answered, finding she neither hated him nor his sophistication, but quite liked him. 'And I did think of driving to Karlovy Vary to. . .' Abruptly she broke off. How could something as important as that have slipped her mind? 'My car!' she exclaimed.

At that moment, however, the housekeeper entered the dining-room, and conversation ceased for the moment while Mrs Novakova exchanged their used dishes for fresh ones. Fabia did note that Ven had a few pleasant words with the hard-working lady before she, smiling, left the room.

Intending not to forget her car again, however, Fabia dipped her spoon into her pudding, sampled it, and discovered it was something of a rather superb plum pie, if different from what she knew.

'What. . .?' she began, and just had to laugh when, not waiting for her to finish, Ven supplied her with his country's name for the dish.

'Švestkový koláč na plech,' he stated, and she would swear that as his eyes rested on her laughing mouth, that the corners of his mouth were picking up too.

She lowered her eyes, took another couple of spoonfuls of her pudding, and then remembered. 'About my car,' she looked up to comment. 'I. . .'

'Ah, yes, your car,' he took over. 'I phoned the

garage today on your behalf,' he went on, and paused, and this time, she, interrupted him.

'And?' she prompted.

'And,' he obliged, after a moment, 'I'm afraid they're having trouble in locating the replacement part needed to get it going again.'

'Oh, lord!' she sighed, but asked hopefully, 'Did they give any indication of how long. . .?'

'It looks as if it could take a week — or more,' he read her question.

Oh, crumbs, she thought, any faint hope she might have nursed of still being able to make it to Prague and Karlovy Vary just gone up in smoke. But, realising that it wasn't very good manners to sit there bemoaning her lot, she made a huge attempt to get over her disappointment, and trotted out lightly, 'Oh well, perhaps it's fortunate that I find Mariánské Lázně quite an enchanting place.'

She was aware of his eyes resting on her and, looking at him, she smiled. She thought she saw a hint of admiration in his eyes, but knew that she was utterly mistaken when, totally impersonally, he said, 'Shall we return to the drawing-room for coffee?'

Fabia quite enjoyed being back in his drawing-room and went to the couch on which she'd sat earlier. It was there that, with a tray of coffee before her, she poured out two cups and handed one to her host, who was seated in an easy-chair at right angles to where she was sitting.

He looked completely relaxed, and she had to own that she felt a little that way herself. Though since she had taken only one glass of wine, she knew that when everything should have been against her feeling in any way relaxed she must thank Ven, and his charm as a host, for the fact that she was feeling so entirely at ease with him.

However, she sipped her coffee and realised that this

really wouldn't do. She was not here to enjoy herself—well, not primarily—but to get that interview under way.

There being no time like the present, Fabia opened her mouth to begin and heard Ven enquire, 'So you think Mariánské Lázně an enchanting place.'

'Oh, yes,' she promptly affirmed.

'What enchants you in particular?' he wanted to know as he downed some of his coffee.

'The architecture, the forests of trees, the very air,' she replied for starters. 'There's just something about the place, I don't know if it's the daffodils about to bud, the horse-chestnuts about to burst into leaf, the colonnade. . .' She broke off, her face rapt as she remembered some of the things she'd seen, some of the things that had got to her. 'Everything—it all adds up to enchantment.'

His look on her face was warm. 'And you haven't seen the singing fountain yet,' he stated, his tone ever so gently mocking.

'Singing fountain?' she enquired.

'It's near the colonnade—but I'm afraid it won't be in action until the first of May—or possibly the last day in April,' he supplied.

'Oh,' she mourned, and, placing her empty cup down on the table, she felt quite disappointed that, come the time for the fountain to be switched on, she would be back in England. 'And does it really sing?' she wanted to find out.

'Sing, no,' he answered. 'Though the mechanics of it are so arranged so that on every odd hour the water plays and the fountain dances in snatches of classical music.'

'Oh, how lovely,' she breathed, her imagination taking off as she pictured the scene in her mind's eye. Then she all at once became aware that Ven was looking at her seriously, all mockery, however gentle, gone, and suddenly she was feeling quite breathless, and discovering that she needed to say something, and quite urgently, to get her over that breathless feeling. 'Hmm — where's Azor, by the way?' she asked off the top of her head.

'You have a passion for dogs,' he stated, his breathing in no way affected, she noted. In fact, his tone was level, and even his expression nowhere near as serious as she had imagined.

'Does it show?' she asked lightly.

'It's not every day that someone wanders on to my property and, when charged at by a Dobermann who'd shot off as I closed the door after us, goes blithely forward and greets it with the words, "Hello, darling",' he replied, reminding her, had she forgotten, that, the dog never far from his control outside of the house, he had soon been on the spot to witness events.

'Um — you like animals too,' she stated, shying away from having the conversation on her.

'How's the ankle?' he enquired, and, causing her heart to palpitate ridiculously, he leaned down and across, and helped himself to her ankle, where a pair of small but pretty blue and greeny yellow bruises were now out.

His touch was as she remembered it, warm and gentle, but as he gently returned her foot to the ground she again felt shy — absurdly and ridiculously shy, when she could never remember being so taken by shyness before — and she just had to look away from him while she collected herself.

The most obvious place to look was her watch, and she studied the dial as if finding it of much interest. Then suddenly, as she started to focus the digits and she read the time, her feeling of shyness rapidly vanished, and she exclaimed in astonishment, 'It's nearly midnight!' she had never, ever known an evening go so quickly, and at once she was on her feet, 'I had no idea. . .' she attempted to apologise if she had over-stayed her welcome.

Ven was on his feet too, his look amused, 'I hope that means you've enjoyed your evening,' he commented smoothly.

'Tremendously,' she told him honestly, and took a step towards the door.

Ven made no move to detain her, not that she had for a second considered that he might. But, leaving her for a brief while, he went to instruct Ivo to drive her back to her hotel, and then escorted her out through the front door.

Fabia was seated in the back of the Mercedes, with Ivo driving down into the valley, when the smile which had been sporting about her mouth suddenly froze. For only then did it come to her that—she *still* hadn't done her interview!

Feeling stunned as that truth hit her, she almost gasped out loud that the whole evening had gone by, a whole evening, and she'd barely asked so much as one of the questions Cara had primed her with! Much less received answers! Indeed, apart from having found out that Ven was unmarried, she had learned precisely nothing!

In fact, as Ivo pulled up at her hotel, she realised that, if anything, Vendelin Gajdusek had learned far more about her that evening than she had ever learned about him!

CHAPTER FOUR

THE next day dawned dully. Fabia awakened and, as she recalled her non-achievement of the previous evening, her mood matched the dull morning.

That dull feeling followed her around as she showered, went down to breakfast, and returned to her room to consider what to do with her day. It was no good blaming her inexperience, she mused glumly. She had as good as thrown her interview opportunity of last night away—Cara would be livid!

Especially, she realised, if Cara got out of her how well her dinner appointment with Ven Gajdusek had gone. Fabia drifted off for a second or two as she recalled the pleasantness of the evening, and the charm of her host. He really was quite something! Those superb dark eyes, that terrific mouth. . . Abruptly Fabia pulled herself together; this was getting her nowhere.

Nor was she going anywhere, another glum thought popped into her head, certainly not Karlovy Vary, nor Prague—not without a car, she wasn't, anyway. But, since she couldn't do anything about the car situation until that wretched part had been delivered, shouldn't she concentrate her worries on what she *could* do something about? Though what could she do? She'd already blown a couple of splendid interview opportunities.

As Fabia saw it then, if she didn't want her sister to heap coals of fire on her head when she got back—and Cara had more than enough on her plate at the moment—then she was going to have to be really pushy and go and ring Ven Gajdusek's doorbell.

74

Instinctively she shied away from that idea, and accepted then that this interview business was nowhere near as easy as Cara had made out that it would be. Fabia was unable to see herself going up to Ven's front door again, but was very aware that she was going to have to make some kind of an effort.

Briefly she toyed with the idea of perhaps ringing Lubor Ondrus, of perhaps inviting him to dine with her at her hotel, and then asking him to approach his employer on her behalf. She scrapped the notion almost immediately. For one thing, it just wasn't in her to get somebody else to do her dirty work. For another — she was remembering the familiar way in which Lubor had put his arm around her yesterday. That, plus that certain gleam in his eyes was enough to tell her that it wouldn't be a very good plan to encourage him.

Fabia took herself off for a walk, but so great were her worries that for once Mariánské Lázně failed to enchant her. She returned to her room and felt so downcast that, choosing a time when she knew that her mother would be in, she phoned Reception for a call to England. She knew as she waited for Reception to ring her back that it could well be, if Cara had been in touch with her parents, that she stood to come off the phone feeling worse than ever. For the only reason Cara would make that contact was, she knew, if Barney was worse.

'Hello, Mum, it's me, Fabia,' she greeted her parent when the connection was made.

'*Fabia, love*, how nice to hear from you!' her mother exclaimed. But, ever concerned for her two daughters, she quickly added, 'You and Cara are all right?'

'Fine, fine,' Fabia as quickly assured her, all she needed to know about Cara and Barney there in her mother's question. Barney was still holding his own. 'I just thought I'd give you a ring.'

'Now isn't that sweet — and just like you,' her mother

replied, without knowing it making Fabia cringe with shame that she too was being served some of the deception she was practising. 'Is Cara there?'

'Not just at the moment,' Fabia squirmed.

'Well give her our love. You're enjoying yourselves?'

'Terrific!' Fabia enthused.

'I'm so glad,' Mrs Kingsdale said cheerfully, 'where are you now?'

'Still in Mariánské Lázně,' Fabia replied, and chatted to her mother for a few more minutes, until her mother promptly gave her another worry to add to her collection.

'We'll see you a week today, then,' she enthused, 'We'll look forward——'

'Actually, Mum. . .' Fabia cut in only then comprehending that to get home by next Wednesday she would have to leave Mariánské Lázně at the latest by Tuesday—always supposing she had her car back, which was doubtful.

'Yes, dear?' her mother prompted.

'Well, actually, this is such a beautiful place, I was thinking of maybe staying on for a few extra days,' she invented hastily, knowing her mother would worry herself silly if she knew the half of it—let alone that her car had packed up. 'That is,' she hurried to add, 'if you and Dad can spare me. . .'

'Of course we can, love, you know that!' Her mother instantly took on the burden of more work without fuss. 'But will Cara want to stay on too?'

Oh, grief. Fabia blenched, caught out, hating having to tell lies but, having started on a path of misleading her parent, forced to go on. 'It—er—depends how—um—busy Barney is,' she made up as she went along, and with relief was let off the hook a little while her mother commented on how hard Barney worked, and how, if he couldn't take his holiday quite as early as he'd planned, that perhaps it might be a good idea for

Cara to stay touring with her, and maybe take a plane to America from Czechoslovakia.

'Though will you be all right driving back on your own?' she fretted.

'Of course,' Fabia adopted a light and confident tone to reassure her. 'But it might not come to that. I just thought I'd find out if I could have the time off—in case.'

Fabia put the phone down having promised that she would telephone again to let her mother know if she was not going to be back in Hawk Lacey by next Wednesday. To her bewilderment, though, she suddenly experienced a most compelling feeling of not wanting to leave Mariánské Lázně next Tuesday!

When Fabia went to bed that night she felt as glum as she had when she had got up. The only bright spot on the horizon as far as she could see was that Barney must have turned the corner and be getting better. Apart from that, everything was the same as it had been—plus. For, now she had telephoned England, it had been brought home to her that she had a couple of choices to worry about. She had to decide before she saw her parents again if she should confess all that she'd been up to. Though no amount of apologising was going to excuse the fact that she had deliberately misled them, even given that she had only misled them from the best of motives—so that they should not worry. She sighed heavily as she realised that either she had to confess or, much worse, she was going to have to continue to lie to them by inventing, when asked, things which she and Cara had done together while touring Czechoslovakia.

And she still hadn't solved the problem yet about what she was going to do about that accursed interview which Cara had entrusted her to carry out! Fabia pulled the duvet up over her head and tried to get some sleep.

Thursday dawned as dully as the day before and

Fabia got out of bed and went through the routine of getting showered and dressed and going down to breakfast with a total lack of enthusiasm or appetite.

She had not long returned to her room however, when her telephone rang, and when she answered it the sun came out. 'Ven Gajdusek,' announced a cool, strong voice she would know anywhere, 'I haven't disturbed you?'

'Not at all,' she replied, feeling at once alive and full to the brim with the enthusiasm which only a minute ago had been nowhere about. 'I'm an early riser,' she added for good measure. 'I've been up ages.'

'Good,' he commented, and, making her heart leap with pleasure, 'I have to drive to Karlovy Vary this morning, and wondered, since you've stated that it was on your itinerary, if you'd like to come with me?'

She tried not to snatch his arm off, and waited all of a second and a half before, 'I'd like to, very much,' she accepted.

Fabia discovered that she still had a broad smile on her face a minute after the call was ended. But that was perfectly natural, she decided. Of course she was smiling—if she handled it right this time, she might be able to ask him point blank for a particular day and time for that—perhaps not so accursed—interview.

She was ready and waiting when Reception rang to say that Mr Gajdusek was there. Dressed in a flared skirt of fine wool which she topped with a shirt and a sweater, Fabia, with a jacket over her arm and too impatient to wait for the lift, hurried down the stairs to meet him.

Which of course excused her sudden breathlessness when she saw him. 'Hello,' she smiled, and, crazily, felt shy!

'Not a lady to keep a man waiting,' he murmured approvingly, and, basking in his appreciation of her promptitude, she went with him to his car and, as he set the Mercedes in motion, had time to realise that she wasn't shy, for goodness' sake. Nervous, perhaps, on edge maybe, because it seemed to her that she would have to keep her wits about her unless she wanted this outing to end up as fruitless as the other times she had been in his company. Nor did she need his approval, about *anything* for heaven's sake!

A minute later, as they left Mariánské Lázně behind, Fabia suddenly started to wonder why the blazes she was being so assertive. Anyone would think she was under threat of something. Grief!

Feeling in no way threatened by Ven, or anybody else, she then began to realise that if she was going to be assertive about anything, then it was about Ven Gajdusek answering one or two questions. Or, to put it more accurately, any fifty of the hundred she'd got lined up.

'Thank you for remembering that I wanted to see Karlovy Vary,' she opened sincerely.

'It's a pity about the rain,' he answered, with reference to the grey cloudy sky.

'It has to rain sometimes,' she stated pleasantly, and loved it when, apparently amused by her philosophical reply, he laughed.

His mouth was even more super when he laughed, she decided, and quickly turned her head to face the front — she could never remember noticing a man's mouth so much before. It seemed a good idea to pin her thoughts elsewhere.

'Have you any brothers or sisters?' she asked, so out of the blue, that she felt as surprised herself as he must be.

Though when she had to turn her head to look at him again, she saw that if he was feeling surprised he wasn't showing it. Then she had the dreadful feeling that he was not going to answer her anyway, for he said nothing. Not until he had negotiated a sudden hazard up ahead; then, apparently seeing no reason why she shouldn't have an answer, he replied, 'I've a brother living in Prague.'

Is he younger or older? Married? Single? Questions arrived in a rush to be asked. But then, as another hazard, this time in the shape of plant machinery on the road, was negotiated, so Fabia saw that it was hardly fair to bombard Ven with questions when he must by far prefer that she keep quiet and leave him to concentrate on his driving.

The pavements were wet when in under an hour they reached Karlovy Vary, but for the moment it had stopped raining. Ven made a brief stop to drop off a parcel at one of the shops in the town, obviously the reason for his having to make the journey. Then, 'Shall we have coffee first before we have a look around?' he suggested, and Fabia immediately felt warm towards him that it wasn't to be a 'straight in and out' trip.

'That sounds a lovely idea,' she accepted, and warmed to Karlovy Vary too with its tree-lined streets and picturesque surroundings.

They took coffee in a smart hotel and, looking at the relaxed Czechoslovakian, Fabia could not help but feel proud to be with him. But, flicking her glance away from him when he caught her looking at him, she formed the view that she must have gone a little light-headed with the guilt of her conscience, because it seemed to her that since knowing him she had been visited by one strange thought or feeling after another.

Time to remember why she was here, she decided firmly, as she banished any crazy light-headed notion that Ven might be responsible for the way her heart fluttered when, looking at him, she found that his eyes were still on her.

'I expect Lubor is busy beavering away back in his office?' she asked as a warm-up question before she got down to basics — and immediately wished that she hadn't because at once Ven's expression darkened, and as he raised an aristocratic eyebrow she knew instantly that all affability was gone.

It was all there in the sharp and arrogant, 'You have a particular interest in my secretary?' with which he flattened her.

'Grief, no!' she exclaimed, and, refusing to be flattened, was a touch uppity herself, she had to own. 'I wouldn't dream of coming between him and his work for you!'

'Good!' he answered curtly. 'Since, however, he is away for a couple of days, there is little possibility of your doing that!'

Pig! she thought, and would seriously have liked to stamp on his foot. She looked away from him and his arrogant aristocratic face, and stared determinedly out of the hotel window. She'd see him in hell before she spoke to him again, she fumed. All she'd done was to make a bit of polite conversation! As far as she was concerned, she wasn't bothered if Lubor never 'beavered away' again. Though, come to think of it, what with Lubor being away for some days last week when she'd arrived, he must have quite some time off from his duties.

Determined not to look at the brute of a man opposite, Fabia was in the act of deciding that she would ask him nothing in future — not even for a ride back to Mariánské Lázně, she'd take a taxi sooner — when she was suddenly brought to an abrupt halt. Oh, hell! For herself, she'd never open her mouth to him again. But there was Cara.

Mutinously she flicked her gaze back to where he was surveying her in stony silence. Damn you, she thought angrily as pride fought a battle with her love for her sister.

Love for her sister won, as in her heart she supposed she'd known that it would. But, even so, pride would not allow Fabia to kowtow to anyone, so that it was in the coolest of tones, her expression wooden and unyielding, that she opened her mouth and asked him bluntly, 'Are you prepared to give me an interview or not?'

My stars — and she'd thought he'd looked arrogant before! Never had any man so looked down his nose at her. She knew then, as he stared at her icily that she was going to be on the receiving end of a straightforward, 'Not,' at any moment now.

But suddenly, even while she was hoping that the hotel would ring for a taxi for her, she saw, she would swear, Ven Gajdusek's mouth twitch. It had been a minuscule movement, but unbelievable as she found it, it had definitely been there. The swine had been amused, she was sure of it! Even though he might be trying to deny it — incredibly, his sense of humour was erupting!

Any smile she might have thought was about to have an airing, however, did not make it. But neither did the refusal she had been so positive about. Instead Ven inclined his head a fraction in her direction and, keeping his face straight, drawled drily, 'You, Fabia, certainly know how to charm a man.'

Her own lips twitched and, even if his smile hadn't made it, try as she might, she couldn't hold hers in. Her mouth picked up at the corners and she just had to laugh. 'I'm sorry,' she apologised, and felt so much better when he, it seemed, couldn't resist grinning. There were ways of asking and ways of asking, and, she accepted, her way *had* been *totally* charmless.

'I'll forgive you,' Ven replied with a wry look.

'And the interview?' she asked nicely before the trail went cold.

'Hmm,' he murmured, but she was glad to see he had lost none of his pleasantness of expression when, considering her request for a few seconds, he divulged, 'After almost two years without a holiday or much free time, I last week completed what I believe to be one of my best achievements.' And while her eyes went wide at the importance of that statement to the literary world, 'It was with no small degree of relief,' he continued, 'that I personally took my work to my publishers in Prague and, that done, resolved that apart from day-to-day correspondence I would have a whole month off — perhaps longer — and free my mind of anything connected with work. Yet now,' his look was amicable, 'you, Miss Kingsdale, with your haughty manner' *her* haughty manner? 'wish me to at once revoke my plans and allow you to ask me endless work-orientated questions.'

Her large eyes were fixed on him, and she wished that she could go away and leave him in peace when he had laboured for so long and so hard. But life, conscience, love of family — it wasn't as easy as that. 'You're saying that you won't allow me to do my interview?' she asked.

'Let us say that for you, and your beautiful green eyes,' he inserted with a sincerity that made her heart stop, 'I will think about it.'

'You certainly know how to charm a girl,' she bounced back at him, and caught his laughing expression full-on, and while her heart danced a merry jig she had to accept that, for the moment, she could forget all about the barely started upon list of questions she had lined up.

Perhaps, though, it was because of his promise that he would think about it, that she saw that as a favourable hope. She was able anyhow, when he suggested they take a walk around Karlovy Vary, to put her worries to one side, and give herself up wholeheartedly to the idea.

Fortunately the rain held off, but walking with Ven, his knowledge of the area seemingly limitless, Fabia doubted that it would have bothered her all that much had the heavens opened.

'Is that smoke?' she asked him, pausing on a bridge to gaze some more, though unable to see any source of a fire. She could only stand and stare spellbound a little when he replied that it wasn't smoke, but vapour from the warm stream that ran through the town.

Karlovy Vary was named after Charles IV, Ven told her, who in the fourteenth century came across the scalding waters of the springs through one of his hunting dogs.

'Scalding?' she questioned, and learned also that temperatures had been known to exceed seventy degrees Celsius.

Having filed that fact away in her head, she was glad of Ven's assistance when, passing a wine store, she asked him if there was a local brew which she could take back to her father. 'There's Becherovka, a liqueur made from the local water and various herbs,' he answered.

'Is it nice?' she wanted to know.

'Rather an acquired taste,' he replied, 'Taken chilled and with ice, it goes down quite well.'

'Then I'll get some,' she decided on the spot, and embarked on a small spending spree, ending up with a bottle of Becherovka, a bottle of plum brandy called Slivovitz and a presentation box of some sweet wafer biscuits called Oplatky which were traditional to the area.

It was not long after that, though, that the rain decided once again to make an appearance and Ven decreed that it was in for the rest of the day. 'We'd better go back to the car,' he announced, and, without more ado placed a hand beneath her elbow and guided her back to his car.

She would have liked to stay longer, but realised that would have been greedy. She would have got soaked

had they stayed any longer, and Ven was quite right to
see it was not sensible to amble around in the pouring
rain. The trouble was, though, that she didn't feel
sensible. Indeed—what the dickens was the matter with
her?—she didn't want to be sensible.

Fabia tried to get her head together as Ven drove
away from Karlovy Vary. She was determinedly con-
centrating her thoughts on all she'd seen, however—
the thermal springs, the cobbled streets, winter
jasmine, not to mention the impressive Mlýnská
Colonnade—when suddenly the question popped into
her thoughts from nowhere: was she, in fact, attracted
to Ven?

Alarmed by that thought, she stared fixedly if unsee-
ingly in front of her. There was no denying, of course,
that he was attractive *plus*, but good grief, she knew
loads of attractive men. Well, perhaps one or two, she
qualified.

A second later and Fabia was wondering what on
earth she was thinking about. Regret not seeing Prague
though she might, perhaps, she began to wonder
whether it was time she returned to England.

There was still her car to worry about, not forgetting
that interview she still had to secure, but. . . Her
thoughts came to a sudden standstill when, to her
embarrassment, her tummy rumbled noisily. Although
she had occasionally missed a meal before and never
heard it protest, it was as if her stomach was asking for
food.

'Forgive me!' Ven took the apology straight out of
her mouth. 'I forgot the hour,' he added, and when
Fabia, glancing at her watch, saw that, incredibly, it
was getting on for three, she realised that when Ven
was working it must be that he didn't give thought to
food. Quite plainly, having so recently finished the
work that had absorbed him for almost two years, he

was not yet back in the habit of eating lunch at a regular hour.

'Forgive me,' she insisted, but was quickly over her small embarrassment, and, feeling as he steered his vehicle up steep hilly, even mountainous terrain that they must be over halfway back to Mariánské Lázně, she suddenly felt completely happy, and just had to tell him, 'I've had a lovely morning. A lovely time,' she added, realising she'd had almost three lovely hours of afternoon time too. 'Thank. . .'

'I like that word, "lovely",' he glanced over to her to state. 'It suits you.' And while her heart swelled — could he be saying that he thought she was lovely? — a few seconds later he was steering the Mercedes around a bend and was then at once driving to the other side of the road where a kind of lay-by had been cut into a high mass of rock. Braking his car, he then turned to her and, again with that devastating charm, 'I cannot return you to your hotel with your insides pleading to be fed,' he stated.

'Oh, but. . .'

She was wasting her breath, she saw, for Ven was already out of the car and coming round to the passenger door. She got out and looked about to see that there across the road, in an area where buildings were few and far between, stood the welcoming sight of a small hotel and restaurant.

A little startled, she looked up, and was more startled because Ven was much closer than she had thought, and she found she was staring straight into a pair of inscrutable and penetrating dark eyes. She saw his glance flick to her mouth, then back to her eyes, and as her heart suddenly started to thunder, so she felt a desperate need to say something — anything.

'Where are we?' she asked on a gulp of breath.

And again had to wonder what the dickens was the matter with her for Ven, in no way similarly affected, moved and, taking casual hold of her arm, began to lead her across the road. 'Bečov,' he replied evenly.

The restaurant was plain and homely, and Fabia, her heartbeats steadying, liked the place immediately. 'Do you often eat here?' she enquired as menu cards were brought to them—in Czechoslovakian.

'It's a pleasant stopping place,' he replied, and Fabia couldn't help it, she just burst out laughing. 'I said something amusing?' Ven enquired, eyeing her laughing mouth appreciatively.

'One of these days you're going to give me a straight answer to a straight question,' she explained, 'and the roof will fall in.'

'So what would you like to eat?' he asked, and she loved it when he grinned. 'Something closely related to English food?' he suggested.

'Certainly not!' she replied indignantly, but felt so good inside that there was no way she could stop her mouth from curving upwards. 'I'd like something typically Czechoslovakian, please, if I may.'

'You want to sample our *knedliky*?' Ven enquired.

'Of course!' she answered promptly. But, as curiosity overcame her, 'Er—what is it?' she had to ask, and saw his eyes light up with laughter.

'Wait and see!' he retorted.

Knedliky, when it arrived, was nothing more sinister than dumplings cut into half-inch-thick slices. Admittedly they did not taste like a British dumpling, but Fabia did not want them to. To go with the *knedliky* Ven had ordered a pork goulash and the two combined were delicious. In fact, as the meal progressed, and Ven good humouredly tucked into his *knedliky* and goulash too, Fabia couldn't help thinking that this was one of the best mealtimes she had ever experienced.

'What would you like to follow?' Ven enquired when he saw she had cleared her plate of every morsel.

'Not another crumb,' she protested, having thoroughly enjoyed her meal, but feeling full to the gunnels.

'If you're sure. . .'

'Don't let me stop you!' she exclaimed quickly when she saw he was about to call for the bill — and immediately wished that she hadn't. Ven was his own man and if he wanted to eat anything more then she was certain that he'd hardly forgo a pudding just because she didn't want one.

Fabia started to breathe again when, in no way put out, 'I've had sufficient,' he replied mildly, and a short while later he escorted her back to the Mercedes.

In the twenty minutes or so it took them to reach the outskirts of Mariánské Lázně, Fabia basked in the warmth of her happy memories of her splendid morning. True, there had been a few unhappy minutes when they'd been having coffee in Karlovy Vary when she and Ven had reared up at each other. Thank goodness, though that for all he wasn't so free with his smiles he had a terrific sense of humour and had not held against her the blunt, not to say impolite way she'd asked if he was prepared to give her an interview.

When Ven drew up outside her hotel, Fabia went on to realise just how kind he had been to give up so much of his time. He had only gone to Karlovy Vary to deliver a package — and look at the time, nearly four o'clock!

She turned to express some of her thanks to him, but he was already out of the car and round by the passenger door opening it for her. Fabia got out, then found that before she could say a word, Ven was escorting her inside the hotel and waiting with her while she collected her room key. From there he walked over to the lifts with her.

'Thank you for a super time,' she offered sincerely as she waited for the lift to arrive — and felt her heart race to beat the band when, all male dark eyes stared down at her.

The lift landed with a 'clump' but as the lift door began to open, 'I enjoyed it too,' he answered gravely, Fabia felt suddenly mesmerised, and his head started to come down. She was hardly breathing when, his lips warm and gentle, he pressed a light kiss to her cheek. '*Ahoj*' he murmured, using the informal version of goodbye, and took a step back.

Like someone sleepwalking, she entered the lift, 'Bye,' she said huskily, and as the lift sailed upwards she wasn't conscious of thinking of anything.

She was still feeling to some degree quite bemused as she walked along to her room. She could still feel the impression of Ven's mouth, warm where he had kissed her, where that super, terrific mouth had actually touched her skin.

She entered her room, but, as reality started to creep in, she suddenly realised that she hadn't said anything more to him about that interview. A smile curved her mouth, though, as she kicked off her shoes and went and lay down on her bed. Because Ven had said he'd think about it. And that had to mean that he'd be in touch again — didn't it?

CHAPTER FIVE

FABIA awoke on Friday with a smile on her face, and lay for some while with thoughts of Ven in her head. He was still there when she showered, dressed and went to partake of what was now her standard breakfast, a flavoursome yoghurt, bread, cheese and coffee.

She was sipping the last of her coffee, however, when it suddenly came to her just how much Ven had been in her thoughts since she had awakened, also how very much she wanted to see him again! Oh, heavens, she thought as her cup went down on its saucer with a clink. For, trying to analyse why she should want to see him again so badly, she realised that the only thing she could be positive of was that her wanting to see him again had nothing whatsoever to do with that infernal interview!

Fabia returned to her room admitting today—where for some unknown reason she hadn't been able to admit yesterday—that yes, she was attracted by him, and yes, she did feel drawn to him.

By the time she had closed her room door behind her, though, while there was still some part of her that didn't want to be attracted to him some other part of her was arguing, Why shouldn't she be attracted to him? With all he'd got going for him, was it any wonder that she should find him more—um—interesting than any man she had ever met?

Twenty minutes went by without her being aware of it. But suddenly she woke up, ousted Ven from her head, and wondered what she should do with her day. It looked like a dull day outside but she couldn't just sit in her room doing nothing. Now if she had her car. . .

Her glance moved over to the phone—should she ring Ven about her car? But he'd plainly told her on Tuesday that it would take a week or more to get the necessary replacement part, so what was the point in ringing him?

It was at that moment that Fabia was shaken to realise that all she was looking for was an excuse to be in touch with him again. Pride in her soared up then and she turned her back on the phone. She was getting ready to go out, however, when, in a flash of unwanted certainty, she knew that there was one very big reason why she shouldn't be attracted to Ven—because he was not attracted to her, and it was all one-sided, that was why!

She did not delude herself that the light touch of his lips to her cheek on parting yesterday meant anything, and she hitched her bag on to her shoulder and walked to the door. Then, the phone in her room rang, and for all of two seconds she stood transfixed.

A second after that and, her heart suddenly racing, Fabia dashed over to the phone—and was sorely disappointed that the call, though an outside one and not Reception, was not from Ven but his secretary.

'Hello, Lubor!' she answered his greeting cheerfully. Why should she take it out on him that he'd got the wrong voice?

'When you would not dine with me on Tuesday, I drove that evening to my parents in Plzeň, but had I known you would sound so pleased to hear me, I would have driven back sooner than last night,' he lost no time in taking advantage. Now, Fabia swiftly realised, was the time to back away.

'How are you?' She ignored his comment.

'Busy,' he replied, and while she bit down a reply of, 'That should keep you out of mischief,' Lubor went on to disappoint her some more, when he added, 'Mr Gajdusek has gone away and left me with very much work.' And while her heart plodded to a dull beat, 'It looks as if I shall have to work the entire weekend,' he stated.

'Well, I expect Mr Gajdusek will give you time off to compensate,' she suggested, holding down more remarks, though in actual fact it was questions which sprang to her lips: where had Mr Gajdusek gone and how long would he be away?

'Of course,' Lubor replied. 'He always does — he's very fair in all his business dealing.'

'That's good,' she murmured, and, her weakened pride taking a dip, 'Mr Gajdusek has gone away, you said?'

'He went to Prague this morning,' Lubor obliged nicely, and then added, 'He particularly asked that, should you have any problems or require assistance in any way, I must make myself available to you.'

'Oh, how kind!' she exclaimed, and felt inordinately pleased that Ven had given a thought to her before he had gone away.

'Do you have any problems?' Lubor asked eagerly.

There was her car, but if Ven couldn't get the garage to get a replacement part before next Tuesday, then she was certain that Lubor couldn't. So, 'None at all,' she replied — though, trying to make her tone barely interested, she just had to ask, 'How long is Mr Gajdusek likely to be away?'

'Who knows?' Lubor answered. 'A week — longer perhaps,' and while Fabia was having disturbing visions of somehow getting her car back and driving home to England and — never mind the interview — never seeing Ven again, Lubor was changing the subject to ask, 'Will you have dinner with me this evening, Fabia?'

She was more than well acquainted with Lubor's proclivity to see an invitation to grow amorous where there was none, though since he couldn't do more than verbally flirt over the dinner table she couldn't see any

harm in accepting. She opened her mouth to suggest
that perhaps she could give him dinner at her hotel —
and thereby eliminate any possibility of him putting his
arm around her in his car — then found that she was
suggesting nothing of the sort, but was asking, 'Did Mr
Gajdusek ask you to invite me out?' and was at once
appalled that, Ven all too clearly not far away in her
head, she had asked such a thing!

But, 'No,' Lubor replied, every bit as if her question
was an everyday one. 'As a matter of interest, he
specifically stressed that I must talk to you on an
impersonal basis only.' And as Fabia gasped at the
implication she saw behind that statement Lubor was
going on, 'It is I who asks you, for myself. On Mr
Gajdusek's behalf, I feel he must mean I am to be
impersonal in any help I give you with your problems.
It is obvious, is it not, that if one gets emotionally
involved in a problem, one cannot perform as well as
when one is viewing it impersonally, yes?'

'Yes,' Fabia agreed, but what was more than obvious
to her, with Ven stressing, 'specifically' stressing, that
Lubor talk to her on an impersonal basis only, was that
he still didn't trust her not to ask personal questions
about *him*. Hurt that he could think she would do that
pest of an interview through Lubor, she was certain
then that she didn't even like Ven Gajdusek — much
less was she attracted to him! As if she'd dream of
approaching Lubor for inside information!

'You haven't yet answered my question,' Lubor
reminded her when, for a brief while, she had forgotten
he had asked it. 'I will take you to a *koliba*, you will
enjoy it very much,' he promised.

'I. . .' She opened her mouth and was ready with her
invitation that they dine at her hotel, but as the thought
that winged in from nowhere that Ven was probably
hitting the high spots in Prague that night — and with
some lovely Czech lady in tow, she wouldn't wonder —

Fabia, with not the least idea of what a *koliba* was, promptly did a switch. 'I'd love to go to a *koliba* with you,' she accepted brightly. 'What time shall I be ready?'

Fabia was ready and waiting when Lubor called for her promptly at six forty-five that evening. 'You are beautiful,' he greeted her with a beaming smile, and raised her flattened spirits, even if she did suppose that he most likely greeted every date that way.

'Thank you, Lubor,' she accepted his compliment graciously just the same.

'I have a taxi waiting,' he stated as he escorted her out of the hotel, explaining, 'It is not permitted to drink and drive at all in Czechoslovakia.'

A *koliba* turned out to be a large wooden chalet-type restaurant which in this case was set amid tall pine trees. Fabia climbed up a flight of steps with Lubor into the timbered, red-and-white-check-curtain-windowed building, and they were shown to a table.

She was still looking admiringly around when, 'I'm so happy that you agreed to dine with me this evening,' Lubor stated warmly.

This Fabia realised, was where the fencing began. 'I've never been to a *koliba*,' she replied.

'You like it?'

'Very much,' she answered, rescuing her right hand which he had suddenly decided to take hold of.

'You have lovely hands,' he murmured, as if to excuse his impetuous reaching across the table for one of them.

'Oh, Lubor!' Fabia chuckled, unable to do anything other than laugh lightly. He was a nice man, and she quite liked him, but where Ven's charm came naturally, Lubor was laying it on with a trowel. The result was that, instead of being swept off her feet as maybe he intended, she found him funny.

He took her amusement in good part, however, and

he took his eyes off her to study the menu for about a minute. Then, as Fabia tried to make sense of the menu written in Czech, he looked across to ask, 'What would you like?'

In all truth, she seemed to have lost her appetite. But, since she was his guest and would have to eat something, she looked hopelessly at the menu again, and smilingly suggested, 'Perhaps you wouldn't mind ordering for me.'

Her order of *polovnický biftek, smažené hranolky* and *velká obloha*, when it arrived, was a plate of steak, chips and vegetables. Both she and Lubor had a glass of beer to go with it, and, having not been hungry, the meal went down much better than Fabia had anticipated. But most of the mealtime was spent with her either backing away from his leading philandering comments, or racking her brain to think of some comments or questions of her own — other than those that so easily sprang to mind, but which all centred around his employer.

There was so much she wanted to ask him about Ven, she discovered. Somehow, she had a need to know all she could about him — and in there lay the conflict — because whatever she would have asked, or learned, was not for any write-up which she might hand over to her sister for her use, but was private and personal, and for her alone.

But she could not ask Lubor anything about the man who attracted her so. Not that Lubor would have answered anyhow. He might be a roaring flirt of the first water, but already she had formed a solid impression that, whatever else Lubor Ondrus might be, he was most loyal to his employer.

While not thinking it fitting to ask him questions about Ven, however, Fabia was wary of asking more than surface polite questions of Lubor himself. He did not need any encouragement at all, as she had discovered when she had lunched with him on Tuesday.

'Have you lived in this area long?' she decided was a safe enough question after a lull when another beer was brought to him.

'Mariánky?' Assuming Mariánky to be a shortened version of Mariánské Lázně, Fabia nodded, and Lubor beamed a smile at her as, 'Only since I have worked for Mr Gajdusek,' he replied, though couldn't resist tacking on, 'It seems that I was meant to come here. . .' he paused for effect, and added '. . .to wait, for you!'

Fabia felt it might be a touch cruel to laugh at him again but, feeling certain he would run a mile if she took him seriously, she was a little nonplussed about how to answer him. She settled for, 'It's been a lovely evening. . .' and was content when he took the hint.

'You would like for us to return to your hotel?'

It was early still, but, while she had quite enjoyed his company and having someone else to converse with in her own language, an early night seemed quite a good idea. 'Do you mind?' she asked.

'It will be my pleasure,' he assured her, and at once left her to order a taxi.

They had arrived back at her hotel, however, before Fabia realised that they were at cross purposes about why she should want to return to her hotel so early. For, apart from trying to hold her hand in the taxi, he had been quite well behaved. She accepted it as perhaps quite natural though when he escorted her inside the hotel and waited with her while she got her key. Ven had done the same thing yesterday.

He had walked over to the lift and waited with her too, she recalled without effort, as Lubor walked to the lift with her and pressed the lift call button. But, as the lift arrived and she turned to bid Lubor goodnight, there any resemblance to Ven and yesterday afternoon abruptly disappeared. For swiftly, and with such adroit-

HOW TO PLAY 421

GREAT FREE GAME
WITHOUT OBLIGATION TO BUY

1 With a coin, scratch the 3 silver dice opposite and discover in an instant whether you will receive... 2, 3 or maybe 4 free books and perhaps 1 or 2 extra gifts.

To claim the Jackpot, it is sufficient that your dice display 4, 2, 1 in any order.

2 When you return the card to us, you will receive as many free Romances as you have revealed and perhaps also a cuddly Teddy and a Mystery Gift.

3 If we don't hear from you within 10 days, we'll send you 6 brand new Romances for just £1.80 each every month. You will of course be under no obligation and may cancel or suspend your subscription at any time by simply dropping us a line.

Mills & Boon Reader Service, Freepost, PO Box 236, Croydon, Surrey. CR9 9EL.
Registered Office: 18-24 Paradise Road, Richmond, Surrey. TW9 1SR
Registered in England No. 100449

Here is the cuddly Teddy that you could receive if you hit the Jackpot!

If you claim your free books we'll also send you this appealing little Teddy absolutely FREE. Soft and cuddly, he's a favourite with everyone.

PLAY 421 WITH MILLS & BOON

Scratch the 3 silver dice and see instantly which gifts you will receive.

YES! Please send me all the free books and gifts to which I am entitled and reserve me a Reader Service subscription. I understand that I am under no obligation to purchase anything ever. if I do not wish to receive 6 brand new Mills & Boon Romances every month for just £1.80 each, I simply write and let you know within 10 days. If I choose to subscribe to the Mills & Boon Reader Service I will receive 6 brand new Romances for just £10.80 every month. There is no charge for postage and packing. I may cancel or suspend my subscription at anytime simply by writing to you. The free books and gifts are mine to keep in anycase. *I am over 18 years of age.*

MS/MRS/MISS/MR _____

ADDRESS _____

POSTCODE _____ SIGNATURE _____

12A3R

**4 FREE BOOKS
+ A CUDDLY TEDDY
AND A MYSTERY GIFT.**

**4 FREE BOOKS
+ A CUDDLY TEDDY.**

3 FREE BOOKS.

2 FREE BOOKS.

**To claim
421 can be in any order**

mps
MAILING
PREFERENCE
SERVICE

THE MILLS & BOON GUARANTEE

- You will not have any obligation to buy.
- You have the right to cancel at any time.
- Your gifts remain for you to keep in any case.

Mills & Boon Reader Service
FREEPOST
P.O. Box 236
Croydon
Surrey
CR9 9EL

TEAR OFF AND POST THIS CARD TODAY!

NO
STAMP
NEEDED

ness that Fabia felt he must have done it many times before, in no time, and before she could blink, Lubor had caught her in his arms. As she moved to push him away, he stepped with her into the lift, pressed the button for her floor, and, as the lift doors closed, he pulled her closer and aimed a kiss at her mouth.

By the time the lift had stopped at her floor, however, Fabia had left him in no doubt that she was not overjoyed by his nerve. 'No!' she told him, outraged. 'Ne!' she gave it to him in Czechoslovakian, and, 'Non! Nyeht!' she endorsed it in French and Russian as well. And, as the lift doors opened, just in case he still hadn't got the message, she gave him one furious push away from her and as he let go of her and went reeling backwards, 'Don't you *ever dare* do that to me again!' she flew. And, while he was still thinking about it, she stormed away from him.

Fabia had been in her room for a good half-hour before she cooled down sufficiently to realise that maybe her reaction to Lubor's hauling her into his arms had been a little — fierce — perhaps. But, yesterday Ven had walked to that same lift with her. Yesterday Ven had gently touched his lips to her cheek — and for Lubor to do what he had just now was an insult to that beautiful memory. And anyhow, she didn't want Lubor to kiss her. In fact, she didn't want any man to kiss her — except. . . Oh, hell! Fabia went to bed.

Fabia was up, dressed and down to breakfast by eight the next morning. She was crossing the foyer intending to return to her room to collect her thoughts, however, when the attentive man from Reception came away from his desk and stopped in front of her.

'There is a telephone call for you, Miss Kingsdale,' he smiled, and quickly added, 'You can take it at the desk if you wish.'

'Thank you,' she answered, hiding beneath a pleasant smile of her own as she went to the desk, that her heartbeats had suddenly picked up speed. 'Hello?' she queried evenly on taking up the receiver—and an instant later, Lubor's apologetic tones hit her ears.

'Fabia, what must you think of me?' he asked, contrition in every syllable.

'Oh, good morning, Lubor,' she answered affably, feeling a mite ashamed herself as she remembered his surprised expression at her furious over-reaction to his unwanted overtures last evening.

'Will you ever forgive me?' he questioned soulfully, and Fabia began to feel a tinge embarrassed, for how, in a public place, could she tell him not to be such an idiot?

'Of course,' she replied lightly.

And immediately wondered if she'd said the right thing, for Lubor wasted no time in asking, 'And what are you going to do today?' In actual fact, Fabia had been wondering that selfsame thing herself. But, while she liked Lubor still, she wasn't sure after last night's performance that she wanted to go out with him again—if that was what he had in mind.

'Um—what are *you* planning to do today?' was the best she could come up with as a counter-remark.

'Me—I have to work,' he replied.

'Oh, yes, you said,' she remembered. Then, as a thought suddenly struck, 'Has Mr Gajdusek taken Azor with him?' she asked.

'Azor!' he seemed surprised by the question. Though after a moment of considering her question, seemed to think that there was no harm in revealing, 'I believe the dog does not take well to city life—he is up at the house.'

'Are you going to the house today,' Fabia wanted to know.

'But of course! I have my office there.'

'Then—do you think it would be possible for me to take Azor for a walk?'

'You want to take that brute for *a walk*?' Clearly Lubor thought she was mad.

'He's gorgeous!' she protested.

'How I wish that I were that dog!' Lubor sighed and Fabia had to laugh.

'May I, do you think?' she pressed.

'You know dogs?'

'We have lots of them at home.'

'Then I will see Ivo, and ask him. He usually walks Azor when his master is not at home.'

Fabia ended the call realising that she was quite looking forward to stretching her legs with Azor. It was another dull day, but, suitably attired, she later went by taxi up to the house.

Her ring at the doorbell was answered by the woman she had seen on her first visit — the one who had spoken a little English. She was a maid, it seemed, by the name of Dagmar, and, 'You will come,' she smiled, and Fabia, realising that she was expected, stepped over the threshold to see Lubor coming from a door a good way up the hall.

'Thank you, Dagmar,' he said to the maid, and all smiles, he took Fabia to find Ivo and Azor.

To Fabia's relief, Ivo had remembered that she had walked the dog with his master last Monday and had observed then, as now, as she gave the Dobermann a light scratch behind one of his ears, that she was totally at ease with the animal.

'I shall be free tonight,' Lubor thought to mention as Ivo handed over Azor and went on his way, and Lubor guided her to a rear door of the house.

'Oh — um — I'm afraid I've scads of letters I must write,' she excused, hoping to be forgiven.

'I make you dislike me?' he questioned, and seemed to be so genuinely distressed at that thought that she felt duty-bound to quickly reassure him.

'Lubor — you're terrific!' she told him, and, Azor

wanting to be away, 'See you!' she added smilingly, and, unleashing the dog, set off.

Azor had been well trained and, even if she didn't know the words of command in Czech, he was an intelligent animal and responded to her tone of voice every time. That being so, he was a joy to walk — which made it odd that she felt as if something was missing. Ven had been there on Monday, of course. Oh, grief, I must be going soft in the head, she thought irritatedly, and concentrated on Azor for the next couple of hours.

Lubor must have seen her returning from his office window, for he was there when she neared the outside door, and, never one to miss an opportunity, 'About tomorrow?' he asked.

'Ring me tomorrow,' she grinned, and, handing him Azor's lead, 'He needs a drink,' she told him, and to Azor, 'Goodbye, you lovely darling,' she crooned.

It was downhill all the way to the hotel, and as such, was easy walking. But, still the same, Fabia felt hot by the time she'd made it to her room, so went and took a shower and changed her clothes and supposed, since it had to be lunchtime, that she should set about getting a snack of some sort.

She was eating a cheese omelette and salad, which she wasn't particularly interested in, when she owned to a feeling of restlessness. Though that was hardly surprising, given her problems. Oh, if only she had her car. That still wouldn't solve the problem of that nightmare of an interview, though, would it?

In remembering that interview, however, Fabia also remembered that Ven had actually thought it necessary to warn Lubor against her asking personal questions about him. And, as that memory hurt yet again, she all at once completely lost her appetite.

She left her meal half-finished and returned to her room to spend quite some minutes in ousting Ven

Gajdusek from her thoughts. Though when, having ousted him, thoughts of him crept back in again, she grew impatient with herself, and took herself off for a walk around town.

She was determined that it wasn't he who had affected her appetite either, and went down to dinner that night and ate quite a substantial meal, only to return to her room and spend the next hour again having trouble ousting the wretched man.

Fabia had just about succeeded when her telephone rang. Lubor, she thought, feeling a trifle guilty that her pen had never touched paper that night. Why he would be ringing, she couldn't think, but when the phone rang again she realised that she would have to answer it.

She picked it up, said a careful, 'Hello,' and then very nearly dropped it. It wasn't Lubor—it was Ven!

'I wasn't sure that I'd find you in,' he drawled for openers—and suddenly Fabia didn't like his tone. Nor did she like his barely hidden insinuation that she was hard-up for a date. And in particular, she did not like at all that he had felt it necessary to give Lubor the instructions he had about her.

And it showed in her own tone when, 'Had you telephoned last night you would not have done so,' she replied coolly, if not a shade haughtily.

'One presumes from that that some male wined and dined you,' he returned, his tone several degrees cooler than hers. Though before she could think of anything sharp by way of a clever answer, 'How many males do you know in Mariánské Lázně?' he enquired coldly.

'Two,' she retorted, 'and the last I heard, one of those was in Prague.'

'He still is!' Ven rapped. And before she could blink, 'Have you seen my secretary today?' he demanded.

And she felt hurt again. All too obviously, Ven Gajdusek didn't want her having any conversation at

all with his secretary. 'He was at the house, when I
went to take Azor for a walk,' she stated stiffly.

'You've been walking my dog!'

'We went miles — do you mind?' The crash in her ear
as his phone went down told her that he did mind — and
very much too!

Only when she stretched out a hand to replace her
own receiver did Fabia realise that she was shaking.
What was all that about? Sinking down on her bed, she
found that it took her quite some time to get herself
more of one piece.

Again and again she went over her conversation with
Ven, and couldn't help but wonder what had got into
her, for goodness' sake! Why had she felt so — so
vulnerable, so edgy with him, that, when Cara was so
desperate for her to do that interview, she had by her
uppity manner just about said goodbye to all chance of
that.

She had no idea why he had telephoned her, though
she didn't put it out of the realms of possibility that,
having gone away when he'd promised to think about
the interview, he might well have rung to suggest some
alternative. Even, perhaps, that he was agreeable to
her asking him her questions over the telephone.

Whatever, she'd ruined all chance of that now, Fabia
realised that. As, ten minutes later, she realised that
she'd be lucky if her sister ever spoke to her again.
Cara had so set her heart, everything, on her doing this
job for her, and she — she had blown it!

For some minutes she again wondered if Cara would
have fared any better. Though since Cara was a professional to her fingertips she supposed that she would.
She wouldn't have upset him by taking his dog for a
walk, that was for sure.

With her spirits at rock bottom, Fabia got ready for
bed. Ven was once more in her head, though, when she
climbed into bed and yearned for sleep.

Around two in the morning she was just nodding off when suddenly her telephone rang again. In an instant Fabia was wide awake and, with a drumming heart, she put on the light.

Ven was her first thought when she picked up the receiver. But then, with shock and pleasure, she heard her sister's voice. 'I thought you might have moved on to Prague. Or have you been and come back again?'

'*Cara*! Oh, I'm so pleased to hear you. Where are you?'

'I'm still in America—and it's just dawned on me that it's probably around midnight where you are. Did I wake you?'

'That doesn't matter. How's Barney?'

'It's been rough. My word, has it been rough,' Cara answered, her tone sobering. 'And although he's much better, the dear love isn't out of the woods yet. But they started him on a new course of treatment yesterday and he's begun to respond.'

'Oh, I'm so pleased,' Fabia replied, and after some minutes of speaking of Barney's condition, 'How are *you*?' she asked.

'I'm fine, a bit tired,' Cara admitted, 'but fine. And you? Are you all right on your own.'

'Of course,' Fabia answered. 'I rang home, by the way.'

'You didn't tell the parents anything about my not being with you, did you?' Cara wanted to know in a hurry, though added more slowly, 'No, you can't have done, or they'd have insisted on you going home straight away.'

'I don't know so much,' Fabia replied, and went on to tell her sister about her car problems and how, because she might not be able to get home by Wednesday, she'd told their mother that because Mariánské Lázně was so beautiful she might stay on longer—and that their mother had assumed Cara might fly to America from Czechoslovakia.

'So that's why you're still in Mariánské Lázně and not Prague,' was Cara's only comment. Then, as efficient as ever, 'You'd better have my phone number here just in case you need to tie up with me on anything,' she decided, and, giving her number, paused only long enough for Fabia to take it down and was then asking, 'Well?'

'Well what?'

'Don't be dumb! What's he like?'

'Vendelin Gajdusek?'

'Who else? How did the interview go? Did you ask him everything I asked you? Did——'

'Cara!' Fabia broke in urgently.

'What?' The word was sharp and Fabia hesitated, and couldn't find the words. 'You didn't lose that list of questions?' she demanded.

'No, of course not.'

'Thank goodness for that!' Cara started on a heartfelt sigh. 'You've asked everything on that list?'

'Well. . .'

'You *haven't*?' Oh crumbs, Cara was sounding a wee bit peeved.

'It's not that,' Fabia began, certain in her heart that she had now scuppered every last chance of that interview with Ven, but with Cara having more than enough to worry about with Barney still so poorly, not wanting to give her something else to be upset about.

'What then?' her sister asked shortly, and, as her quick brain clicked, 'You haven't lost your own notes?' she made a guess.

'No!' Fabia denied—she hadn't any to lose!

'You messed the interview up then didn't you?' she challenged, her tone urgent. 'Hell's teeth, Fabia, the least you could have done for me was to. . .'

'I haven't messed the interview up. . .' Fabia tried to

get in, though before she could add—because there wasn't any interview—Cara was cutting in.

'I'm sorry. I'm sure you've done a super interview for me. I'm not thinking straight,' she further apologised. 'What with missing sleep and everything else, my nerves are more than a bit wrung-out, I'm afraid.'

'Would you like me to come out to you?' Fabia at once volunteered, her heart aching for her sister.

'Good lord, no. I'm all right, it's just, with that interview meaning so much to me and everything else, I just wanted to know that I could forget all about it, and concentrate all my energies on Barney.'

'I understand,' Fabia told her, and, guilty though she felt, she knew then that until Barney was 'out of the woods' she wouldn't be confessing to her her failure to secure the interview.

'I'd better go,' Cara began to end her call. 'I'm sorry you've missed seeing Prague—but you're otherwise having a good time, aren't you?'

'Great!' Fabia told her enthusiastically, said goodbye, and replaced the phone, to stare bleakly and unseeing in front of her.

Great! What could be greater? Her car had broken down, she had as good as lied to her parents, and had somehow managed to offend the man whom her sister would bend over backwards not to offend—and now she had just practically told Cara, when there wasn't the remotest chance of it happening, that the damnable interview was in the bag.

Great! She couldn't wait to wake up tomorrow to see what disaster that day would bring!

CHAPTER SIX

AFTER a restless few hours' sleep, Fabia awakened to daylight and the concrete knowledge that for her sister's sake she could not accept defeat on that interview issue. For Cara, she simply *must* try again.

How any attempt was going to be made when she was in Mariánské Lázně and Ven in Prague, she hadn't fathomed as she made her way down to breakfast. But she knew then that, plagued and plagued again by the same thought during her fretful waking night-time hours, she just could not leave it.

So OK, without too much effort she had offended Ven Gajdusek, it seemed, but he most definitely had said he would think about giving her the interview! And, whether he was on holiday or not, whether she had offended him or not, that still left the interview question open—didn't it?

With the light of morning she just couldn't allow herself to believe, as she fully had last night after his phone call, that she had blown all chance of an interview, and Fabia sipped her coffee and wondered—how? How, when she was where she was, and he was where he was, was she going to achieve what must be achieved? Where did she start?

After about ten minutes of deliberation, Fabia could plainly see that there was only one place to start, and that was to put through a call to Lubor in the hope that Ven had phoned him too last night. Perhaps he had given him some idea of when he would be home. There was no guarantee, of course, that Lubor would tell her if he had. But, to her way of thinking, and bearing in mind Lubor's loyalty to his employer, it surely couldn't be considered disloyal to give her a hint of when he would be back from Prague.

Fabia returned to her room, but her faint hopes were already getting fainter. What if Lubor said he had heard, but that Ven wasn't returning for another week? A moment later, though, and she was bringing herself up short. What if it was a week; she could wait, couldn't she? She was going nowhere without her car, was she? At that point, she realised that she must take a more positive attitude.

Five minutes later, being positive had brought her to the decision that since time was going to drag heavily while she waited in Mariánské Lázně for Ven to return, and since they had trains in Czechoslovakia, she would go to Prague too. The possibility of bumping into Ven in Prague was more than remote, she knew that. Though so much the better if she did. However, since she needed to fill her time until his return, what better way than to go to the capital city, and spend some days taking a look round?

She felt better for having made that decision; perhaps her car would be ready by the time she came back. She'd have to ring her parents, of course, to let them know that she was definitely extending her holiday. But, for now. . .she took the letter bearing Ven's address and telephone number from her bag.

She left it until after ten to phone Reception to get her call, hoping with all she had now her decision was made that Lubor was so busy that he would be working this Sunday.

When her call came through, however, and she picked up the phone and said, 'Hello,' she realised that she wouldn't have to ask Lubor when Ven was coming back — because she already knew. For it was Ven's voice that answered her!

She gasped in surprise, her heart suddenly started to race and, while her mind went blank, Fabia couldn't think of a thing to say. That was until, '*You're* calling me!' Ven drawled.

'Oh, yes,' she quickly woke up at his reminder. 'Er—though actually I was ringing to speak with Lubor.'

'You wish to speak with my secretary?' he enquired coldly, his tones suddenly clinking with icy hostility.

Again Fabia was reminded how this man must really think she would go behind his back to get information about him from his secretary, and her heart settled to an angry beat. But she couldn't afford to be angry—or to offend him again, she realised, and took a deep and calming breath. She was under control when, in pleasant tones, she stated, 'To be more exact, I'd intended to speak to Lubor to enquire if he'd any idea when you might be returning from Prague.'

Silence was her answer, but just when her anxieties began to spiral again, 'You wanted to see me?' Ven enquired evenly.

'Yes,' she replied—and, taking the plunge, 'Well, you said. . .' Her voice tailed off. But she mustn't lose this moment, she knew that she must not. 'About the interview. . .' she attempted—and got snarled at for her trouble.

'It's suddenly urgent?' he slammed back at her—and Fabia could cheerfully have hit him.

He was being annoying on purpose, she fumed, but, aware that this man easily had her emotions all over the place, she again strove for calm. 'The thing is, I was thinking of going to Prague myself,' she hung grimly on to her self-control to get started again. 'But if you could give me some minutes of your time, I'd happily delay my visit,' she suggested—and silently added, or not go to Prague at all.

A lengthy pause was her reply. But with her emotions out of gear yet again, she hung in there and hoped that whatever he said next would be favourable.

Though, when he did speak, it was not of the

detestation of an interview at all, but to enquire loftily, 'How do you plan to get to Prague — they've returned your car?'

'Not yet,' she replied, realising from that comment that he must have informed the garage of her name and the hotel she was staying at. 'But I can take a train. I've only to. . .'

'I think we can do better than that,' he returned smoothly, and, making her heart spurt with activity again, 'I've merely returned home for some papers. I shall be driving back to Prague myself this afternoon.'

'Oh?' she questioned carefully, while her brain was rattling off the clamouring question — was he saying that he would give her a lift?

'Are you booked in anywhere?' he went on to enquire before she could sort out any kind of an answer.

'Er — no but. . .'

'You'll find it impossible to do so at such short notice,' he commented. But, even while her spirits were taking a nosedive that, supposing he was offering her a lift to Prague, there wouldn't be any point in accepting if it was unlikely she'd be able to book in anywhere, he, to her absolute astonishment, was going on, 'There's a spare room in a suite I've reserved for this month — you can have that if you wish.'

'I can. . .?' she gasped. Oh, grief — this was all *too much*! Her brain patterns seemed to go all haywire then, but as once more Fabia got herself back together, so that most important matter she had to think about rose to the surface. Yet she sensed that now was not the time to press for a formal interview. Now above all times, she felt, was not the time to push her luck. So, 'Thank you,' she said quickly. 'That's very kind of you.'

'Be ready at two!' he instructed — and terminated her call.

Minutes afterwards, Fabia was still sitting stunned and hardly able to credit that she was going to Prague with Vendelin Gajdusek—that he was allowing her to use a spare room in his Prague hotel suite!

She was still feeling somewhat shaken an hour later— she was going to Prague—and with Ven!—when suddenly she realised that she'd barely moved since that phone call. She had better get a move on, she realised. Ven would love it if, though he'd given her ample time, she kept him waiting.

Fabia got busy with her packing and, that done, she went down to Reception to pay her bill. When she informed the man on duty that she would be back shortly, however, but didn't know exactly when, it was he who suggested she might wish to leave some of her luggage in the hotel's store. 'Why, thank you,' she accepted, and, thinking it an excellent idea, she returned to her room to rearrange her suitcases to take to Prague with her only that which she thought she would need.

By ten to two she had deposited the larger of her two suitcases, had partaken of a cheese sandwich and a cup of coffee and, seated in the hotel lounge, and with time to kill while she waited for Ven, she was again being plagued by the vexed question of that abominable interview. She wondered then, since Ven was proving so elusive, whether she should take the opportunity on what she estimated would be just under a hundred-mile drive to Prague to get in there with some of Cara's questions.

Recalling, though, how on the drive to Karlovy Vary she had decided against bombarding him with questions so that he could concentrate on his driving, Fabia, with some reluctance, faced the fact that that was the only course to follow. It was hardly fair, was it, to fire one question after another at him from the moment she got into his car at Mariánské Lázně until she got out again in Prague? Especially when the traffic towards the city was probably extremely busy. But to ask him those questions soon was essential. Cara had made it sound so easy when she'd said 'All I'm asking is that you bring me back relevant facts and answers'. Just *trying* to put some of those questions to the man was turning the whole ill-fated interview into a monster that dominated a good deal of her thinking.

But—suddenly Fabia had had enough. Not that she would let Cara down; she could never do that. But for the moment she resolved that she would not think of the loathsome interview again until she was in Prague. She had no idea of course how frequently she might bump into Ven in the short while in which she shared his suite. But, she determined then, at some time she must most definitely find some space in which to tackle the issue with him.

She was watching the door when on the stroke of two the tall Czechoslovakian came striding into the hotel. But even as her heart, for no known reason, gave a ridiculous flutter, he saw her and came over.

'Just the one?' he asked easily, taking up her case just as she reached for it.

'I'm leaving the other one here,' she replied.

'Then we'll go,' he stated, and, placing his hand on her upper arm, he escorted her out to his car.

'How long will it take us to get there?' she asked conversationally as they left Mariánské Lázně behind.

'Not long. Two hours at the most,' he answered, conversational himself. 'Have you ever holidayed in Prague before?'

'No, never,' she replied.

'Nor travelled to the city for the purposes of your work?' he thought to enquire, a reasonable enough question in the circumstance of his thinking her a journalist, she realised. But as feelings of guilt suddenly swamped her, only then did Fabia appreciate how much she had been herself with Ven. Somehow—though how when it bothered her so—she had all too frequently

managed to forget that she was supposed to be Cara
Kingsdale, professional journalist.

'No,' she answered quietly, and felt so guilt-ridden
then that she couldn't look at him, but turned her head
and stared out of the side-window.

That feeling of guilt sat heavily with her for most of
the drive to Prague. Only then did she see that she
should never have accepted Ven's invitation. It wasn't
right. It was deceiving him. He thought that she was
someone else and would — and justifiably — be furious if
he ever found out. It was no good saying in her defence
that she'd only meant to be Cara Kingsdale for an hour,
because things hadn't worked out that way. And
anyhow, it was still deception, be it only for a minute.
She had accepted his invitation under false pretences,
and that was deception — and she had an instinctive
feeling that Ven was a man who would abhor deception — and would take her apart if he ever found out.
All she could hope, therefore, was that he never did
find out.

'We're coming into Prague now,' Ven remarked
suddenly, and Fabia stirred herself to look about her.

'Everything's more forward here,' she noticed, as
they went by a line of horse-chestnut trees that were
leafy and about a month in advance of those in
Mariánské Lázně.

'I think you'll find it warmer too,' he replied, and
soon after that he was drawing up outside their hotel.

Formalities did not take long, and in no time they
were riding upwards in the lift and then walking along
a corridor to the door of Ven's suite. This door led to a
large entrance lobby, to the right of which stood a
luxurious bathroom, while to the left was a range of
built-in wardrobes. In the centre of the lobby was
another door and, moving forward, Fabia stepped
through the doorway and into a comfortably furnished
large sitting-room.

A porter had already been up to the suite with their luggage, she noted, as she observed that off the sitting-room — with French windows to a balcony between — were two other doors.

'You're in here,' Ven remarked, taking up her case and heading for the door on the left of the French windows — and as she followed him into a pleasant bedroom, 'With luck, by the time you've unpacked, the waiter will be here with some tea.'

'Tea?' she questioned witlessly.

'I thought I'd better prove that I don't always forget about normal times for refreshing the inner man,' he drawled, but there was such a twinkle in his eyes, so much charm in his manner, that Fabia felt quite overcome by it. Her eyes smiled up at him, her mouth smiled up at him. She saw his glance flick down to her mouth, then abruptly he was turning away. His tone was still pleasant though when, as he walked from her room, 'We'll take tea in the sitting-room,' he invited.

She caught herself smiling ridiculously when he'd gone, and realised that she felt quite cheered that he hadn't simply given her a lift to Prague, seen her safely installed in the spare bedroom, and then forgotten about her.

Fabia then got busy with her unpacking. She knew, as she carried articles that required hanging up through to the wardrobes, that she was not going to tresspass any further on Ven's generosity than to partake of a cup of tea with him. But as she returned to her room and closed the door, she silently thanked him that, when rather than encroach on his privacy she might have kept to her room, he had on their arrival thought to invite her to share his sitting-room for half an hour.

There was a chest of drawers in her room, and she had just finished folding away other articles of clothing when she heard voices in the sitting-room. Then she heard an outer door close, and guessed that refreshment had been delivered.

Fabia felt a nibble of excitement get to her as she ran a comb through her long golden hair, and even found that there were traces of a smile picking up the corners of her mouth. On that instant she put down her comb, and turned her back on her dressing-table mirror — and at the same time rejected any notion that she felt in any way excited. She wouldn't mind a cup of tea, of course. Indeed, now she came to think about it, she felt quite thirsty. But when, for goodness' sake, had anyone ever got excited at the prospect of a cup of tea?

That crazy notion disposed of, Fabia left her room, saw that Ven was already in the sitting-room, and her smile came out again. Well, why wouldn't it? she questioned as she went and took a seat on the settee in front of the tea-tray — she was in Prague, and she felt happy.

'Shall I be mother?' she looked at Ven to enquire.

'Pardon?'

'I'm sorry,' she swiftly apologised, when she could see he couldn't make head or tail of what she was talking about. 'It's an expression meaning, "Shall I pour?",' she added in a rush, with a glance to the teapot.

'That's a relief,' he replied drolly, but there was amusement in his eyes, she was glad to note, and as he took an easy-chair opposite he requested, 'Please do.'

Fabia poured a couple of cups of tea and handed Ven his. 'Cake?' she enquired, observing how completely relaxed he looked leant back in his chair, with his long legs stretched out in front of him. He shook his head, but she found the delicious-looking cakes too irresistible, and just had to sample the gooiest-looking one of all. Then, as she glanced up, she saw that, amusement still in his eyes, Ven had been watching her. 'I'm a glutton?' she enquired.

'Anything but,' he replied, as if remembering her dainty appetite when she had dined at his home. 'I was just wondering how, when a few women of my acquaintance would shrink in horror from such a confection, you manage to down such delights, while at the same time maintain such a slender and perfect shape.'

Fabia was well pleased that Ven thought her shape perfect, though she wasn't sure how she felt about the 'women of his acquaintance'. But, because she liked him, she smiled, and answered honestly. 'Some days I walk miles — that could have something to do with it.'

'You walk to your London office in preference to using your car on your non-interviewing days?' he enquired, and Fabia looked swiftly down at the carpet.

Oh, heavens, she thought as guilt again swamped her, she was going to have to be much more careful. Just see how, in quite innocent conversation, she could so easily trip up!

'Talking of interviews——' She raised her head to smile. 'Well, I know you're on holiday and everything,' she rushed over one hurdle to take on another, 'and I really don't want to intrude, but you said. . .'

'I said I would think about it,' Ven cut in, but she was pleased to see that he was relaxed still, and in no way hostile at her bringing the subject up again. 'As you have so rightly reminded me,' he went on, 'I am on holiday; so for that matter are you.' And, with a hint of a smile playing around his mouth, 'Before too long, Fabia, I shall make a point of discussing an interview with you. But, in the meanwhile,' that hint of a smile deepened, 'I must insist that we both forget work, and enjoy a period of respite.'

'Oh,' she murmured. What she had been after was a specified date and time. But Ven, who must be feeling drained from his labours, had just stated that he would be ready to discuss the interview soon — she somehow knew then that she was not going to get a better offer from him than that. On the holiday side of it—well, from her point of view she could do with a respite from thinking about that interview. It *would* be a holiday to discard the worry of it for a few days. In fact, she was feeling lighter-hearted already. She could spend a few days in Prague just enjoying herself, and. . .'

'You agree?' Ven interrupted her thoughts.

She knew she hadn't any choice anyhow but to agree. But, 'Yes, of course,' she gave in graciously, and was rewarded when his smile did make it.

'Good!' he commented briefly, and then, to her immense surprise, 'I suggest we dine about eight, which. . .'

'*We*!' she exclaimed.

'You object to the idea?'

'No, but. . .'

'Good!' he repeated. 'I'll arrange a taxi for seven-thirty, and——'

'But. . .' she cut in, and could see that he thought that to cut in was his sole prerogative when his look became stern and hostile. 'But,' she ploughed on never-theless to protest, 'this is *your* holiday! You don't have to take me to dinner!'

At once all sternness and hostility fell from him and, amusement lighting his dark eyes once more, 'I *do* know that, Fabia,' he drawled, adding, with pole-axing charm, 'Believe me, I wouldn't take you anywhere, did I not want to.'

Oh, heavens—was he something, or was he some-thing? 'Then—thank you,' she replied quietly, and, although she had washed her hair only yesterday, she decided that she just had to wash it again. 'If you'll excuse me,' she requested, 'I've a couple of things to attend to.'

By seven-fifteen that evening, she was ready and, as that nibble of excitement she had experienced before started to get to her again, she took a look in her mirror for reassurance. Ven Gajdusek was a man of some sophistication. She hoped he would approve of her smart black dress and the way she had pulled her hair back from her face and pinned it in a classical knot at the back of her head.

Not that she had dressed that way especially for him, she hastily denied. She occasionally did style her hair that way and, since she had never so much as dreamt of meeting Ven when she'd purchased her black dress, no one could suggest that she had bought it with him in mind.

Why was she making excuses anyway? she scoffed, as a flick of a glance to the small and feminine watch on her wrist showed she should leave her room to be ready to go down for when the taxi arrived. She didn't need to make excuses; it was natural, and only good manners surely, that as Ven's guest she should try to look her best.

That she was looking her best, or that Ven appreciated her appearance was made thrillingly clear a minute later, when she entered the sitting-room. For he was already in there, tall and immaculate in a superbly cut suit.

'Hello,' she murmured, and felt unaccountably shy for a moment.

'Hello yourself, Fabia Kingsdale,' Ven murmured, and, coming over to her, he stood and silently surveyed her in her smart black dress, her sophisticated hairstyle, her flawless complexion, and her fine bone-structure. Then, 'I thought you beautiful before,' he remarked quietly, his sincere dark eyes now fixed on her large green ones. 'But beautiful is an understatement.'

Fabia opened her mouth to make some kind of sophisticated reply, but her heart was racing so much — nobody had even paid her such an extravagant compliment before, and yet made it sound true and sincere, and not extravagant at all — that she could think of nothing to say. Which left her drowning, and groping for words—and only able merely to reply huskily, 'Thank you, Ven.'

For a moment more his eyes held hers, then, as if paying homage to her beauty, and with such elegance of manner that she felt quite spellbound, he took hold of one of her hands, and raised it to his lips. 'Shall we go?' he suggested evenly.

By the time the taxi had delivered them to the restaurant Fabia was feeling on more of an even keel. But even so, as Ven escorted her inside to where he had a table booked, she felt him a most potent force.

The dining-room was high-ceilinged, glittered with antique crystal chandeliers, and had an air of discreet gentility—and from then on the evening simply flew by. The service was good, the food well above average, and her escort. . .? He was a man, she discovered again, who was extremely good company, who could talk on any given subject and make one want to hear more, and whom it was a pleasure to be with.

She began her meal with a few *hors-d'oeuvres*, with the caviare one tasting particularly good. She then had a delectable mushroom soup—and for the main course she chose something that was entirely new to her. *Vařené hovĕví se žloutkovou sýrovou omáčkou*, which was boiled beef with a cheese and egg yolk sauce, served with rice, went down very well, but left her with little room for more than an ice-cream afterwards. By the time coffee was served, however, Fabia was feeling enchanted, intoxicated—and it had nothing to do with the glass of South Moravian Vavřinecké, which she'd taken with her main course. Ven, she knew full well, was the cause. He had made her laugh several times, had laughed once at something she'd said, she recalled, and the entire evening had gone by on winged feet.

And to crown it all, 'What a charming companion

you have been,' Ven commented across the table as he waited for the waiter to bring him their bill.

Me! she wanted to exclaim, because from where she viewed it it had been Ven, with his natural charm, who had been the charming companion. 'I've had a splendid time,' she replied instead, and when some minutes later a taxi whisked them back to their hotel she felt it had been a dream of an evening.

'Something to drink before you go to bed?' Ven offered as they walked in through the door of his suite.

Oh, how she was tempted! But, while there was a great urge in her to want to extend the dream of an evening, there was also that part of her that, for all Ven's, 'I wouldn't take you anywhere, did I not want to' and his 'What a charming companion you've been', caused her to push temptation away. He had been more than good as it was; she really must not trespass on his hospitality. So, 'Thank you, but I think I'll turn in now,' she refused politely. Though added, most sincerely, 'And thank you too, for a lovely evening.'

'It was my pleasure,' he replied urbanely, and added, 'Goodnight, Fabia.'

'Goodnight,' she answered, and went swiftly to her room, to spend some minutes leaning against the door with a dreamy smile on her face.

Some minutes later she heard the sound of a door quietly closing, and guessed that Ven, not bothering with a nightcap seemingly, had gone to bed. Which wasn't such a bad idea, she realised, and moved from the door.

For modesty's sake she got out of her clothes and into her night clothes, and, taking her black dress with her, she left her room, crossed the sitting-room, and hung her dress in the spacious wardrobes in the lobby. Then she went and took a quick shower.

She was still dreaming of her lovely evening though when, showered, dried and back in her night attire, she left the bathroom and opened the sitting-room door, went in—and stopped dead. Ven, a book in one hand and a Scotch in the other, had just entered the room from his room.

Suddenly then Fabia became overwhelmingly conscious of her thin cotton robe, her scrubbed face with her hair, brushed out of its knot, now floating around her—and it all at once seemed more urgent that she return to her room with all speed.

So, 'Goodnight,' she bade him a second time, her goodnight this time, however, sounding husky and hasty as she started to hurry back to her room.

Somehow though—with Ven moving forward too, she realised it wasn't so unexpected—she met him in the centre of the room. She halted, hesitated, flicked a glance at him and saw from the surprised look on his face that he was putting his own interpretation on why she was scurrying to her room.

Nor, Ven being the man he was, did he waste any time in giving his thoughts an airing. For, all in the instant of his book and glass being set down on a nearby table 'You're afraid of me, Fabia?' he demanded to know in a straightforward, no nonsense manner.

'Afraid of you!' she gasped, and, truly horrified that he could think such a thing, 'No, of course not!' she faced him squarely to state. Though, since her denial was hardly any excuse for the way she had been trying to bolt to her room, she felt honour-bound to give him just as straightforward an explanation. 'I—um—think I'm a bit—um—shy,' she managed to own, feeling no end of an idiot.

'Shy?' Ven queried, as well he might, she realised, for she'd been chatting to him like a veritable magpie all evening with not so much as a hint of shyness.

'I—er—think it must be shyness. That or. . .' She broke off, and looked at him helplessly, then saw in his face a look that said, while he was thankful that she wasn't afraid of him, he was doing his best to try to comprehend. 'I know it's crackers,' she told him unhappily, 'but I'm just not used to trotting around in my nightclothes with. . .'

She had no need to go further for, with one eyebrow going aloft, 'With a strange man about the place?' Ven, comprehension there, finished for her.

'Well—um—you're not so strange,' she attempted a joke to lighten the atmosphere, though owned, 'but you've got the general idea.'

'I see,' he commented slowly. But then, clearly startled as some thought came to him, a sudden exclamation in his own language rent the air, and, 'Would I be right in thinking that no man, known to you *or* a recent stranger, has ever seen you ready for bed?' he asked.

It was a quaint way of putting it, but Fabia knew what he was asking. 'Well—my father, of course,' she somehow felt a shy need to prevaricate. But on looking into Ven's no-nonsense dark eyes, she just had to answer his question truthfully. 'Yes,' she said simply.

'You're a virgin?'

'Well, I don't usually go around telling the world,' she mumbled, feeling slightly awkward, 'but—um—yes.'

'Oh, Fabia,' Ven murmured swiftly, and his look suddenly filled with understanding. 'Sweet one, don't be embarrassed,' he added gently, and, bending forward, he placed a tender, almost reverential kiss on her brow.

'Oh!' she whispered, something about his kiss, his touch, moving her. She could still feel the imprint on her brow.

'Goodnight, little one,' he bade her softly, and Fabia was suddenly in a dream world again. A dream world where, this time, she wanted him to be in no doubt whatsoever that she was unafraid of him. His kiss to

her forehead, she rather felt, gave her leave to show
him just how unafraid of him she was.

So, 'Goodnight, Ven,' she bade him for a third time,
only this time she stretched up to him and touched her
lips to his cheek.

Suddenly though, for all she pulled back, she just
didn't seem capable of moving away from him. Suddenly, she just wanted to stay close. Indeed, their
bodies were brushing each other when Ven raised an
arm and, as if meaning to turn her away from him in
the direction she must go, placed it around her
shoulder.

But she didn't go. For he didn't turn her. And that
arm about her shoulders all at once tightened. And
suddenly, instead of turning her away from him — he
was drawing her towards him. And she — she went
willingly.

Fabia was holding on to him as much as Ven was
holding on to her when their lips met. And oh, she
inwardly sighed, and wanted to be nearer to him. Ven's
kiss was deep and satisfying but, as he broke that kiss
and his eyes burned into hers, she wanted more.

A moment's fear smote her then that he might leave
it at just one kiss, and with more daring than she had
known she possessed she leaned her lightly clad body
against him. She heard a groan leave him, and in the
next moment his mouth was over hers again, and he
was pulling her yet closer to him, his hand warm at her
back, moulding her to him.

'Ven!' she moaned, when he released her mouth
from his, but delighted in his touch when he traced
feather-light kisses down her throat and to the low
neckline of her nightdress. When his mouth returned to
capture hers, she was in heaven again, and lost count
of how many kisses they shared after that.

She felt his hands, warm and caressing, moving from
the back of her, and was in a land of breath-held

enchantment when his moving, caressing fingers
stroked and captured her full, throbbing breasts. She
wasn't sure that she didn't cry out his name again.

Then, as if the cotton of her nightdress was a hin-
drance to him, she felt his fingers busy at the ribbon
ties at the shoulders. Only then did she become conscious that its matching wrap was no longer wrapped
around her. But then it was that thoughts began to
penetrate her desire-clouded mind — the realisation
that, should these ribbon ties become undone, then her
nightdress would fall straight to the floor — and she
would be left — stark naked.

'No!' she cried on a sudden note of panic, and backed
a step from him.

On the instant, as if she were a hot coal, his hands
dropped away from her. 'It's all right! I won't harm
you!' Ven swiftly reassured her, and — even while it was
dawning on her how he was accepting her 'no' without
question when she had been giving him a 'yes, yes, yes'
for the past five minutes, he was reaching for her wrap.
Taking it from the arm of the chair where he had tossed
it, he handed it to her and put some more space
between them. Then, as she quickly shrugged into it,
he stated evenly 'Despite how it looks, Fabia, I didn't
bring you to Prague to seduce you.'

'I know that!' she exclaimed in quick and certain
reply, because though everything was such an uproar in
her head, she was positive about that if nothing else.

He looked pleased at her reply, she saw. There was
a hint of a smile on his face anyhow when, 'I think,
then, my dear, that as far as possible you'd better keep
your distance from me,' he stated.

And that pleased her! 'Goodnight!' she wished him
for a fourth time, and went to her room feeling very
much better about everything. Because when, without
so much as a scrap of protest, Ven had let go of her just

now, she had started to get the idea that perhaps he hadn't desired her anywhere near as much as she had wanted him.

But, surely, for him to say that if she didn't want to be seduced, she'd better keep her distance had to mean that he really did desire her — didn't it?

CHAPTER SEVEN

ANY feelings of shyness Fabia might have endured the following morning at the thought of seeing Ven again were shortlived when she did actually see him. He was clad in a short towelling robe, and his hair was damp, and he was clearly on his way back from taking a shower when, on her way to carry out her own ablutions, she passed him in the sitting-room.

'See you for breakfast in half an hour,' he greeted her.

'You're on,' she agreed, adding as she went by what her phrase-book had assured her was the correct greeting for early morning, *'Dobré ráno!'*

He did not answer but just before she heard his bedroom door close she would swear that she heard a small chortle of laughter — as if her dry afterthought of a good morning had amused him.

Fabia smiled, and discovered as she stood under the shower, that she was cheerfully humming a snatch of one of Dvořák's *Humoresques*.

She hadn't realised that they were going to breakfast in the suite or even that she would share breakfast with him. But when, having returned to her room, she presented herself, trouser-and-shirt-clad and with her long shining hair neatly groomed, it was to discover that Room Service had paid them a visit. There was a dining-table against one wall in the room and it was now covered in a snowy white tablecloth and held all the trappings of breakfast.

'Hungry?' Ven enquired, pulling out a chair for her at the table.

'I don't know how I dare confess it after that meal

125

last night, but yes,' she admitted, privately thinking that in casual trousers, shirt and sweater Ven was certainly a man to make one's pulses race.

'What are you going to do today?' he enquired, joining her at the table as without further ceremony they got on with breakfast.

'As much as I can,' she laughed as she poured them both a cup of coffee.

'Sightseeing?'

She nodded, and asked, 'Where's the best place to start?' — and hardly dared to believe his reply.

For, 'I'll come with you if you like,' he offered lightly.

'You'll come. . .' Oh, wouldn't that be too wonderful! 'Oh, but you don't want to. . .' she began to deny, but her voice faded when she saw one eyebrow ascend — as if it was unheard-of for anyone to tell him what he wanted or did not want to do. 'I'm sorry,' she immediately apologised, but, because she just couldn't believe that he truly meant to tramp the streets of Prague with her, 'Honestly?' she enquired eagerly.

His grin, his devastating grin said it all. And as her heart turned over, so she again remembered his, 'Believe me, I wouldn't take you anywhere did I not want to' of yesterday. And it would be a case of him taking her sightseeing if he went with her wouldn't it? And she knew it for a fact when he murmured smoothly, 'I think I might find it agreeable.'

They did not dawdle after breakfast, and while Fabia went to her room to add a lightweight sweater, a jacket and her shoulder-bag to her ensemble, Ven went to his room for a jacket. Ten minutes later they were walking away from their hotel.

Prague was a very old city, built on seven hills, and there was much to see. But the whole while, as Ven took her first to the Hradčanské Náměstí area — a square noted for its preserved medieval ground plan — Fabia was overwhelmingly conscious of him.

She was barely aware of other tourists as the sound of their feet rang out on the cobbled streets, and over the following hours Fabia was deep in everything there was to see apart from the castle and the National Gallery with its collection of old and new European art. Most spectacular in her view, and built in the courtyard of Prague Castle, was the fourteenth-century St Vitus' Cathedral.

But there was so much else to see that, as time flew by, it was no surprise to her that, having been thoroughly absorbed, she had forgotten entirely such necessities as eating, until Ven good-humouredly mentioned, 'Since I didn't wish to intrude on your pleasure to suggest a coffee-break, will you permit me, at ten past one, to suggest we have a break for lunch?'

'It's never that time!' she exclaimed, witnessing a smile playing around his mouth. And, while her heart raced that there was a hint in what he'd just said that he might be prepared to sightsee with her that afternoon, 'You must be parched!' she apologised.

'All in a good cause,' he commented with more of his inbuilt charm, but firmly took her away from things Baroque or Gothic by hailing a passing taxi.

The taxi took them off to a small restaurant, and with everywhere seeming crowded to full capacity Fabia guessed, when they were straight away shown to a table, that Ven must have had the forethought to book in advance.

'Well?' he enquired, once they were seated.

'What would I like to eat?' she queried, thinking that that was what he meant. But he shook his head.

'What do you think of Prague?' he elucidated.

'In a word—fantastic!' she replied, and would have trotted out all she'd seen again, had not a waiter come along and placed a menu in her hands. '*Děkuji*,' she remembered her Czechoslovakian thank-you, and smiled at the waiter—and just then caught Ven's eyes on her. It did funny things to her insides — she thought it was about time to study the menu.

'Have you decided?' Ven queried laconically some seven or eight minutes later.

Fabia took a deep breath and plunged. 'If it's not anything too absolutely awful, I think I'll try the *Špíz ze srnčiho či jeleního masa*,' she answered, without having the least idea of what she was ordering.

'Strange,' Ven drawled, 'I was going to order the same,' he added solemnly, and, not giving her a hint of what she had requested, he passed their two orders over to the waiter.

To her great relief, however, Fabia subsequently discovered that she had asked for a quite delicious meal of venison with bacon, mushrooms and tomatoes. It was no wonder that the corners of her mouth should twitch upwards in her relief, she felt — though her smile became an absolute grin when, flicking a glance across at Ven, she caught his mouth twitching upwards too.

A second or two later, however, Fabia was turning her concentration to her plate, and giving herself something of a silent talking-to — her theme being that Ven would think he was lunching with some deranged lunatic if she went on grinning like that at him all through the meal. She could not deny, though, that she was feeling extremely happy that Monday.

She tried however to pin her thoughts on other matters and, recalling that Ven had only returned to Mariánské Lázně in order to pick up some papers, she realised that, since they were important enough for him to make the four-hour return journey, he must want them to hand over to someone else. It was on the tip of her tongue then to ask if he had managed to dispatch the papers to whoever they were destined for, but she held back the question before it got uttered. The last thing she wanted him to think was that she was prying into that which did not concern her. But, in any case, it was obvious, since she hadn't seen him hand any envelope over to anyone, that he must have sent his important papers off with a messenger when she was either in her room or in the bathroom.

'What would you like to see this afternoon?' Ven enquired as they came to the end of the meal.

'You don't mind?' she asked, thinking it more than good of him to use his morning squiring her around, without him letting himself in for an afternoon of more of the same!

'I should be delighted,' he replied urbanely, and, if he was stretching the truth, Fabia could not tell.

'There's an astronomical clock I've. . .' she began, but needed to say no more, for Ven was already cutting in.

'Then we must go to the *Staré Město*,' he informed her.

'*Staré Město*?'

'Old town,' he translated. 'It's the oldest quarter in Prague,' he went on, 'dating back to the thirteenth century.'

It was just coming up to three o'clock when the taxi dropped them off in the old town square and Ven guided her to the old town hall where, with barely a minute to go before the run-through of the astronomical clock, Fabia stood in rapt attention. She was entirely unaware that the man she was with was watching her enchanted face and not the spectacle she was so taken with. The lower part of the horloge, the round calendarium, depicted the course of village life, and the signs of the zodiac. Above that, and also circular, was a complicated sphere measuring time and showing earth, moon and sun between the signs of the zodiac. Above that were two windows which opened every hour and a procession of Apostles appeared in each window. Fabia was watching absolutely fascinated when, in a window above these other two windows, the run was completed by a golden cockerel shaking its wings and crowing.

'Wasn't that terrific?' she turned to Ven to eagerly exclaim—and felt her heart begin to race yet again when, his expression somehow gentle, he did not speak for a moment but just stood and looked at her.

A second or two later though and she realised that she must have been mistaken, for his look was suddenly more mocking than anything when, 'In a word,' he lobbed back at her, 'fantastic.'

Her heart steadied and, deciding that she quite liked being teased by him, she smiled. 'Thank you, anyway—it *was* great!' She rather thought then that they would be returning to their hotel, and, because she had enjoyed everything so much, she added sincerely, 'And thank you for taking me around, and for showing me so much.' But she was to experience yet more joy, since it seemed they were not to go back to their hotel straight away.

For, 'While there's a lot we haven't touched on yet—no visit to Prague is complete until you've walked over the Charles Bridge,' Ven told her.

'It—isn't?'

He shook his head, and really whetted her appetite by hinting, 'We are so close to it, we could walk there in less than ten minutes.'

'Are we going to?' she asked, ready by then to beg him if need be.

But that wasn't necessary, for, looking down into her earnest face, 'Of course,' he replied, good-humouredly.

Fabia felt that she would remember forever crossing—with Ven—the bridge that led to Prague's Little Town quarter, Malá Strana. Prague was divided in two by the river Vltava, with sixteen bridges linking the two halves. But the Charles Bridge, with it brick-laid walkway and towering Gothic gateways, was the oldest. Though it was not only the bridge and its impressive

Baroque sculptures that Fabia found so memorable, but incidentals such as seeing swans on the river, or the feel of Ven's hand on her elbow guiding her, or standing with her while she watched artists at work, or a man playing a violin, and hearing a flute being played somewhere while a trinket-seller sold his wares. And, most gloriously of all, how the sun suddenly decided to appear — and at that same moment a blackbird started to sing its heart out.

'There's no need to ask if you enjoyed that,' Ven commented as they left the bridge and he looked down into her eyes, which were shining with pleasure.

'Fantastic just isn't good enough,' she replied quietly, and felt at one with him, and the world.

She began to feel a little differently, though when less than an hour later they entered Ven's hotel suite and as she turned, about to give him her polite but none the less sincere thanks as they halted in the middle of the room, Ven looked down at her and got in first with, 'Are you tired?'

It was a reasonable enough question, she thought, considering that they must have walked miles that day. But somehow she didn't feel in the least tired, and shook her head. Looking up at him, 'It's been such a marvellous day,' she replied, openly, honestly, — but suddenly, as his glance pinned hers, she felt unable to look away. More, she felt that Ven was feeling rather the same himself!

Which all went to prove how totally wrong she could be when in the next instant Ven swung abruptly away from her and informed her coolly, 'I've an engagement this evening. Will you mind dining on your own?'

Several emotions battered her at once then, so how she managed to find a voice that was as cool as his she would never know. 'Of course not!' she replied, and even found a cheerful note from somewhere to add lightly, 'I ate a huge meal at lunchtime, so I'll probably have a snack sent up,' and, making for her room before her emotions tripped her up, 'You've been more than kind as it is. Thank you, Ven,' she added affably and escaped to her room.. . . . feeling *furious*!

She did not enter the sitting-room again until she was certain that he had gone out. She hoped he enjoyed himself! She didn't care a hoot, for goodness' sake, that he had an 'engagement' that evening. Nor was she in the least bit jealous about whoever his engagement was with—but she'd lay odds it wasn't with his Prague-residing brother!

It annoyed her intensely that she should have thought for a moment that the dreadful feeling she'd experienced when he'd told her he had an engagement was jealousy. Huh! As if she cared. No, what she found so overwhelmingly infuriating was that when he had enquired tactfully, some might say, whether she was tired, he clearly had been expecting her to say a polite 'yes' so that he could then suggest that she had an early night. Well, to the devil with him! Just let him mention sight-seeing tomorrow, that was all!

Fabia did not sleep well that night and, though Ven returned quietly in the early hours of Tuesday morning, she was awake, and heard him coming in.

She had no intention whatsoever of breakfasting with him, though, and stayed in her room for as long as she could bear it. But she had risen early and found that staying put with nothing to do was growing more and more irksome.

This is ridiculous! she fumed crossly, and without more ado snatched up her toilet-bag and went to her door and listened. When she could hear not a sound she went swiftly from her room, through the sitting-room, and into the bathroom.

Naturally, despite being an early riser, if yesterday was anything to go by, *he* was still snoring his head off, she explained away why she had seen nothing of him.

No doubt, too, he was dreaming pleasant dreams of his dinner companion of last night!

Oh, hell! she thought, and, furious with herself as much as him suddenly that her thoughts alone could make her so angry, she turned the shower on full force and tried to drown her thoughts that way.

Half an hour later, her cotton wrap once more about her, though with a towel about her shoulders, Fabia, with her long newly washed hair clinging wetly to her, emerged from the bathroom.

As luck would have it, when she was certain that, shiny-faced and wet-headed, she must look about her worst, it was at that moment that the outer door opened and Ven came in.

For a startled second Fabia could think of nothing to say—but not so Ven. Even while it was registering on her from the newspapers in his hands that he was no lie-a-bed but was up and had been out for his paper, he was taking in the damp, startled look of her and, feigning surprise himself, 'It's a mermaid!' he declared.

What could she do? She laughed. 'Good morning!' she offered, but felt suddenly so light-hearted, she couldn't believe she had but minutes earlier been so cross, and went quickly to her room to hurriedly get her hairdrier into action.

Contrary to her firm intention of not breakfasting with Ven, however, since he was standing by the table which was set for two when she again entered the sitting-room, she thought it would be infantile in the extreme to carry on with that intention. Especially when Ven seemed not only to be waiting breakfast for her, but actually pulled out a chair for her.

'Thank you,' some treacherous inner person she had only recently become acquainted with trotted out courteously as she took her seat.

'Any plans for today?' he enquired as he accepted the cup of coffee she poured for him.

'I. . .' she began, and was suddenly afraid that this new-discovered, not-to-be-relied-upon inner person might yet weaken last night's resolution that, should he offer to sightsee with her today, she would tell him what he could do with his offer. 'I. . .um — not sightseeing,' the part of her that was made of sterner stuff cancelled out all chance of such an offer.

'Good!' Ven promptly replied. 'I'm in favour of a walk around some greenery myself,' he stated, and casually threw in, 'Care to come?'

A walk around some greenery wasn't sightseeing, was it? Nobody could say it was, tugged that treacherous inner self. 'That sounds a lovely idea,' she found she had answered before she had given herself time to think further.

She wasn't unhappy with that decision, she owned when later she and Ven left their hotel. In fact, she was feeling much more cheered than she had been. So much so that she was able to quieten any last lingering niggles about how easily she'd folded by telling herself that tomorrow she would, most definitely, go out on her own. Tomorrow, she promised — not of course that Ven was likely to want to accompany her anywhere for a third day in a row — but tomorrow she would insist on going sightseeing on her own. She hadn't seen Wenceslas Square yet, she itemised, and to see the square named after the patron saint of the Bohemian kingdom was surely a must for any visitor to Prague!

Having, however, decided upon that course, Fabia felt yet more light-headed, and gave herself up to the pleasure of her walk with Ven.

He took her to Petřín Hill, an area of parkland with a funicular which climbed to the top from where splendid views were to be seen. 'It's so peaceful here!' Fabia exclaimed as, more strolling than anything, they ambled along hilltop pathways through an avenue of silver birch trees.

'I thought you might like it,' he commented, and Fabia had to give her special attention to catkins, and to where lilac was about to break out of bud, because as her heart began to race she couldn't help but think that Ven had intended to bring her with him to Petřín, even as he'd casually tossed that invitation at her.

Suddenly then though her attention was taken by a red squirrel which darted from nowhere and, effortlessly it seemed, bounced over the grass and then, as if jerked up on a string, shot up a tree. 'Oh, look!' she whispered in an awed kind of voice, and flicked a glance from the squirrel to Ven, to find that he was looking—at her!

'Nature-lover,' he teased, and she knew then that she held him in some quite high regard.

After that the morning was absolutely crowded with sights, sounds, and to Fabia even the very air seemed perfumed. There was a rose garden to wander around, though as yet no sign of blossom but an indication from the many rose bushes that at some time there would be a most beautiful display. The May blossom was out, however, and there was green everywhere, in lawns and trees, and in shrubs and bushes, together with purple pansies and statues, while in the background birds sang.

As had happened the day before, the time simply flew for Fabia, so that she could again hardly believe it when Ven told her that they would take the funicular a little way down the hill to a restaurant where they would have lunch.

Nebozízek seemed to be the only stop the funicular made before going on down to the bottom of the hill. But they alighted at Nebozízek. Though before they could reach the restaurant they had to first go down some concrete steps, and then up several flights more.

What Fabia ate that lunchtime, though, she barely knew. Somehow she suddenly felt so overwhelmingly aware of Ven that, while recognising that she was eating beef of some kind, food as such seemed incidental.

When they left the restaurant they stood for some moments surveying the view of Prague, its many spires, red-roofed buildings, with a green dome here, the Vltava river with some of its bridges there, the Charles Bridge in particular Then, 'Shall we walk the rest of the way down?' Ven enquired.

'Please,' she replied, but she was grateful to him that he did not hurry her but allowed her to look her fill before they set off through a pathway of more trees and green parkland.

Fabia was conscious of Ven every step of the way, but tried her hardest to concentrate her thoughts else-where. She succeeded to some extent when a most magnificent full-blossomed magnolia tree caught her eye. And the next moment, nearer at hand, there was a statue of a man with the name of Karel Hynek Mácha on the plinth beneath. But what attracted her attention most was the fact that several single flowers — a red tulip, a yellow one, a carnation — had been laid at the statue.

'Who was he?' she just had to stop and ask.

'A poet. A romantic poet.' Ven halted too, and, seeing that Fabia was interested, he went on to tell her of Mácha's best known poem, called *Maj*. 'Or, May — not that it needs a lot of translating,' he commented.

'May — the month?'

'The same,' he replied. 'Mácha gloried in nature's beauty in May, though his poem marks the difference of the solemn quietness of love in nature, and the passion of human love.'

Something began to well up in Fabia then as she looked at Ven, and her breath caught. But struggling manfully,   'And — er — he's   very   popular   in Czechoslovakia?' she asked.

'Especially to those under the enchantment of love,'

he answered, and Fabia experienced a need to discover if Ven himself knew or had ever known that enchantment.

But she couldn't ask, and she looked away from him, her glance falling on the flowers on the poet Mácha's statue. Then, even as it dawned on her that the flowers had probably been placed there by lovers, so, as she looked up again into the dark eyes of the tall Czechoslovakian, she all at once knew why it was that her breath had caught a few seconds ago. Indeed, why it was that she felt so breathless now. Because then it was that she knew, with blinding clarity, what had been there for some time now. She did not merely like him, did not merely hold him in high regard; she was in love with him! Devastatingly so. Though what enchantment there was to be found in that love, she failed to see. Because by no stretch of the imagination would Ven ever come to love her!

CHAPTER EIGHT

THE one, two, three and then four hours since she had acknowledged her love for Ven alternately dawdled and then flew for Fabia. Ven had invited her to dine out with him that night and she had accepted. But now, with only a little while to go before she must join him in the sitting-room, she was starting to have second thoughts about the wisdom of accepting.

She wanted to dine with him, of course she did — but that was just the trouble. It was because she knew that before the month was out she would have said a permanent goodbye to him that she was greedy to spend as much time with him as she could now.

But her acknowledgement of her feelings for him was still new, and even while wanting to be with him she felt nervous, terrified that by some small look or too-ready smile she might give away her feelings — that she didn't want to say that goodbye — and that to do so would break her heart.

There was about a minute to go before she should pin a friendly, but nothing more, type of smile on her face and leave her room. And that was when her conscience, which because she'd got something else to think about had stayed quiet, suddenly started to get to her about the way in which she was deceiving the man she loved.

Feeling thoroughly disquieted, she left her room in a rush. Ven was leaving his room at just the same time, and, 'Hello,' she offered in a friendly, bright way, and was stabbed at by fingers of conscience all the way down in the lift.

Oh, how could she deceive him when she loved him

so much? How could she not when there was Cara?
'Are you all right?' Ven enquired and she realised that
some small groan of despair must have left her.

'Perfectly,' she replied, and preceded him out of the
lift very much aware that, no matter how conscience
and love might insist that she make a clean breast of
everything, to confess was something she simply could
not do. He would be furious, of course, and rightly so.
But, even if she could find the nerve to admit to her
deception, she couldn't own up to a thing—Cara was
depending on her!

Fabia was seated beside Ven in a taxi when she
realised that furious would be an understatement for
what Ven would be if he ever learned that she had not
only deceived him but, to add insult to injury, allowed
him, believing her to be someone else, to house her
and feed her into the bargain.

Such thoughts were poor stimulus for a conscience-
stricken appetite, and although the restaurant which
Ven took her to was smart, and the food good, Fabia
was able to eat only little. She said even less and was,
in fact, having the utmost difficulty in trying to be
natural with him. Luckily, though, Ven, while well-
mannered throughout, seemed to her to be otherwise a
shade preoccupied.

'Your steak's all right?' he enquired courteously,
when at one point he observed that she wasn't making
much headway with it.

'Fine,' she replied lightly, and feeling in the need of
some excuse, 'I had a big lunch,' she added, though
was having amnesia about what she'd had at lunchtime.

It was something of a relief, however, that when she
had finished a final small ice-cream, and drunk a cup of
coffee, Ven called for the bill. She was still struggling
to adjust to this love, this, the biggest happening of her
life. But she also needed to come to terms with the
topsy-turviness of her situation that, while she wanted

to spend every moment she could with Ven, she suddenly felt a need to be alone!

She was to get her latter requirement quicker than she realised, she discovered. For no sooner had the taxi dropped them off at their hotel, and Ven had escorted her inside, than, 'If you'll excuse me, Fabia, I have someone to see,' he stated evenly — and suddenly she was feeling dreadful on a couple more counts.

'Of course,' she replied smilingly, and didn't need him to wait with her by the lift or to see her safely inside.

In fact, as the lift sailed upwards, she its sole occupant she was feeling quite put out by Mr Vendelin Gajdusek. So OK, she hadn't been the best dinner companion in the world that evening, but *she* hadn't asked *him* to take her out, *he* had asked *her*. Quite clearly, though, he could hardly wait until they got back to their hotel before he dumped her.

Fabia reached Ven's suite and let herself in, walked across the sitting-room and into her bedroom where she sat down on the edge of the bed, and felt, for the moment, defeated. Love, she was swiftly realising, was hell — being in love was hell! For, while her pride was up in arms that plainly Ven would have preferred to take someone else out to dinner — had that 'someone else' been free — what was really getting to Fabia was nothing but common-or-garden, out-and-out jealousy.

Well, good luck to him! she fumed, as she shot from the bed, collected her toilet-bag and night attire and went furiously to the bathroom to take a shower. The night was still young, so whoever the female was who worked peculiar hours, or whatever the reason was that he couldn't have seen her earlier — and by then Fabia was certain that 'someone he had to see' would be female — then she hoped he had a truly lovely time!

Fifteen minutes later, however, and Fabia's anger, like her shower water, had drained away, and she was feeling unhappier than she ever had in her life. She went back to her room and, leaving a small bedside lamp on, she switched off the main light and got into bed.

She did not aim for sleep, though, but lay there for an age wanting some of her anger back. She needed that anger, it helped her to cope. Without it, she was racked by a feeling of utter desolation.

Fabia had no idea of how long she lay there feeling beaten, but, as she put out her small light and closed her eyes, she just didn't need to have anything more land on her plate of despair. But it was then that her conscience started to plague her once more. Oh, no, she silently grieved, and as her conscience prodded away at her until she was in an agitated state of mental uproar, so all her disquieted spirits urged that the next time she saw Ven she must confess the whole of it to him. How could she, though? An anguished groan escaped her, the certain knowledge hers that both she and Cara could say goodbye to that interview for ever if she breathed a word of the truth to him.

At that moment a violent thunderstorm began outside, and as rain started to lash her windows and thunder and lightning crashed about so Fabia pulled the bedclothes over her head. Some time later, with the storm still going on, Fabia, with her conscience overburdened with guilt, fell into a tortured sleep.

It was not, therefore, surprising that her dreams should be likewise troubled. Nor, with the man she loved so much in her mind, that Ven should feature largely in her troubled dreams. Ven was in danger! She stirred restlessly. She must help him! She had to go to him! She moved violently in her sleep—and started to come to the surface of that sleep, just as, outside the hotel, there was a sudden screech of tyres on tarmac as brakes were slammed on.

In the next second there was a sound of metal hitting

metal, and in the next instant, Fabia was out of bed and heading for the door. Ven! She had to go and help Ven!

In a very few moments she was racing from her room and into the sitting-room. And light suddenly hit her eyes and she halted, blinked, and only then became conscious that Ven wasn't in danger at all.

'Something is wrong, Fabia?' he asked urgently, leaving his stance over by the French window where he must have been taking a look outside, to come over to her.

'I—er. . .' She faltered, and fought desperately to get her head together. Ven wasn't in danger, nor whatever the time was, was he in bed. But, fully clothed, he must have been reading in the sitting-room—or maybe he had just come in—when he too had heard the sound of a car crash. 'I think I was dreaming,' she mumbled, and, all at once feeling no end foolish, she looked up, wanting to apologise or something, but mainly wanting to get back to her room with some kind of dignity.

Though as her sleep-filled eyes met Ven's dark ones she realised that there was no sign there that Ven thought her foolish. If anything, there was something almost tender in his look when, 'Poor *drahá*,' he murmured gently, while at the same time he moved a hand to where her shoulder-strap had fallen down, and put it back in place again.

Fabia knew then that, a semblance of dignity hers, she could now go back to her room. But—just his touch on her arm made her skin tingle and, besides, she liked him tender, gentle like this. And, whatever it was that *drahá* meant, she liked that too.

So, while that sane part of her made her half turn as though to return to her bedroom, that other part of her, the part that tingled and loved him, caused her then to delay—just for a moment. 'W-was there a car crash—or did I dream it?' she asked softly.

'It wasn't a dream,' he replied, and, as if to assist her on her way, he placed one arm around her all but naked shoulders and took a step with her towards her room.

'Is anyone hurt, do you think?' she asked, feeling all shaky inside from just his touch.

'From the way both drivers got out from their vehicles and looked ready to tear each other apart, I doubt it,' Ven answered, and halted at her bedroom door.

This was where she bade him a pleasant goodnight, Fabia knew, and she fully intended to do just that. Only she looked up first into his eyes, and again saw that his eyes were gentle. She opened her mouth, but the word 'goodnight' wouldn't come and then, almost imperceptibly, though she was sure she felt it, his arm about her shoulders tightened fractionally. 'Oh, Ven,' she cried, and the next she knew was that his arm about her had definitely tightened. More, that his other arm was coming about her to encircle her too.

The kiss they shared was a mutual one. A kiss where she raised her lips to his, and he did not hold back from moving his head down to hers, and, as her heart started to sing, so her arms went up and around him.

Gone were her troubled thoughts, her troubled dreams. In fact, as she clung to him while they shared another kiss, and then another, she wasn't thinking at all. And, as Ven shrugged out of his jacket, the closer to get to her, if she was dreaming then she never wanted to wake up.

'Fabia!' he breathed as she leaned her thin-cotton-clad body against him.

'Ven!' she whispered, and was barely aware that they had moved to the darkened area of her bedroom.

The light from outside, and the light from the sitting-room shone through to her room as Ven moved with her to her bed and sat down there with her. 'Beautiful, Fabia!' he murmured, and with his hands warm at her back, he traced tender kisses down the side of her face.

She groaned aloud in pleasure when his kisses continued down to the swell of her bosom. But this time she had no objection to make whatsoever when tenderly, unhurriedly he undid first one shoulder-strap, and then the other. Then, with his eyes fixed on hers, in the light that was shining through to the bed, he gently let the material of her only covering fall down to below her waist.

'*Moje milá*,' he gently breathed, and, pulling a little away from her, he looked down to the naked swollen pink-tipped breasts he had uncovered. An exclamation in his own language left him then. But, 'Oh, my dear,' he followed on, and tenderly, with one finger, he traced the outline of her left breast.

'Oh, Ven!' She shuddered in pleasure, in wanting, as that finger caressed to the hardened peak he had created. And as both his hands moved and he gently cupped her breasts in his warm hold as though each were infinitely precious, a sigh of bliss, of need left her. 'I want to feel you too,' she murmured, a hint of shyness entering her tones.

But, to her great delight, Ven not only heard her husky words, but understood, and, with a kind of discreet gentility, he laid his mouth gently on hers, and while she returned his kiss and started to burn and ache inside for him, he discarded more of his clothing.

When next Fabia put her arms around him, it was to discover, to her further rapture, that Ven's shirt had gone. She wanted to cry his name aloud again, but his mouth was against hers, his hair-roughened chest against the naked globes of her breasts, and she loved him, wanted him, needed him and, as he moved her until her back was on her mattress, she had no objection to make when he removed her only covering from her altogether.

'You're so exquisite,' he murmured throatily and bent down to trace kisses from her belly up to her mouth.

Oh, my darling, darling, she wanted to cry, and as he moved and lay down with her and their legs entwined, so she realised, without fear, that along with his shirt, so too had his trousers gone.

'Ven!' she cried his name joyously aloud, and knew that soon he would make her his.

And to be his was what she wanted—which made it such a nonsense that when, as he caressed his hands over her naked behind and then pulled her to him, that as her body came into contact with the pure maleness of him, she experienced a moment of totally unexpected panic. 'Oh!' she exclaimed and, pulled back from him. But her action was only momentary, and, 'I'm sorry,' she whispered almost at once. And so that Ven should know how truly sorry she was, she held on to him with both arms and tried to pull him to her. But—the damage was done, and Ven, resisted!

And when he suddenly rolled away from her, she was absolutely horrified. Feeling shaken rigid, she watched him move to sit on the side of the bed when, to her further distress, even while his breathing was ragged, she saw him grab up his shirt and trousers.

'I said I was sorry!' she gasped urgently. 'Please, Ven,' she begged, her body aching for him.

Some hoarse Czech expletive rent the air, then 'Forget it!' he snarled, and was already getting into his trousers.

'Forget it?' she echoed, stunned. 'But what. . .? Did I do something wrong?' she asked, instinctively seeming to know then that there was something more at fault here now than her unexpected moment of shy panic.

'I'll say,' Ven snarled, and was over by the door,

blocking out the light from the sitting-room when, 'I never did like my women *that* clinging!' he barked brutally.

Fabia was still staring witlessly at the door after he had quietly closed it behind him. In fact, she was still lying where he had left her, in shock, bruised, wounded, and still trying to take it in when some minutes later, in the still of the night, she heard the outer door of the hotel suite close. Ven had gone out!

A riot of other emotions raged through Fabia then, eventually ousted by shock that he could do what he'd done, say what he'd said and then—calmly leave! The swine, the pig, the rat! How dared he do this to her! How dared he take her up to heaven and then drop her—just like that?

Fabia was still feeling outraged when, listening for Ven's return, an hour passed and she had heard no sound of him. No doubt he had gone to arms that were *less* clinging, she fumed jealously, irately. Well, to *hell* with you, sweetheart, she railed, and, her pride once more up in arms, a certainty in her head that she had seen the last of Ven for that night, she rocketed from her bed, took a shower, and got dressed.

'*Clinging*!' Cara or no Cara, she'd had it! Getting out her suitcase, and with her fury riding high, she began throwing her belongings into it—she was catching the first plane out of there!

Daylight was just around the corner however, but by the time daylight did arrive, although she and her pride were very much certain that she'd see Vendelin Gajdusek in hell before she ever spoke to him again, certain other practicalities had entered her head.

Her other suitcase was back at the hotel in Mariánské Lázně. But while she would be quite prepared to forget all about it—what about her car? It had been her parents' eighteenth birthday present to her. They were bound to ask a *few* questions!

Feeling hurt, and wanting to lick her wounds in private, another sort of pride came to Fabia then. A pride that decreed that no one, and that included her parents, should know how much she was hurting, bleeding inside.

Collapsing down on to the edge of her bed, Fabia gave her situation several minutes' thought. But, no matter how much she wished to avoid returning to Mariánské Lázně, the answer kept coming back again and again that *that* was her only option.

She took a dull sense of relief from the fact that she need not see Ven Gajdusek again. Though fate laughed hollowly at her elbow when she recalled that, from the harsh way he had left her, he'd be doing his utmost to avoid accidentally bumping into her anyway.

In any event, if luck was on her side, and by her reckoning it was high time luck paid her a visit, the garage might well have delivered her car to her hotel by now — or at least have telephoned to say that it was ready for collection.

Fabia snapped her suitcase shut and rang down to Reception for some help with train times. With a bit more luck, train services willing, she could be in and out of Mariánské Lázně today, and, even if she had to fit in a visit to that garage near Františkovy Lázně, by nightfall she could be across the Czechoslovakian border and on her way home to England.

Before eight o'clock that morning Fabia had left the hotel and was at Prague railway station. At eight forty-seven her train for Mariánské Lázně moved off. Stage one of her mission completed, reaction set in, and she could have howled her eyes out.

The train was due to arrive at her destination at midday — which gave Fabia, free of any other occupation, ample time to go over and over again everything that had happened.

She had been clinging when she'd been in Ven's

arms, she had to admit that, but then—she loved him. He didn't love her, of course, not that she expected him to, but he hadn't been backward in the lovemaking department, had he? What did he expect, for goodness' sake!

For the next hour Fabia was alternately angry that he could take her to such heights only to call a halt when she responded too readily, and despair that he had made such a nonsense of her that she hadn't known where the dickens she was.

She tried to pin her thoughts elsewhere, but found that they always boomeranged back. She thought of other happenings since she had arrived in Czechoslovakia, and concentrated her thoughts on Lubor—who hadn't found her clinging enough. Her thoughts annoyingly flitted back to Ven again, and she realised now, of course, just why she had been so outraged when Lubor had tried to kiss her last Friday. She must have been in love with Ven even then without knowing it. Lubor's lips weren't the right lips and subconsciously she had known it. It just wasn't right!

Ven Gajdusek had no such finer feelings, of course, either conscious or subconscious. He didn't give a fig about her, and to prove it he had, in all probability, gone from her bed to kiss some other woman!

Because of some delay or other—line workings, Fabia rather thought—her train was late pulling into Mariánské Lázně, and it had gone twelve-thirty before she was ensconced in a taxi and on her way to the hotel which she had left—was it only three days ago?

If she was feeling totally devastated as she re-entered the hotel she had left last Sunday, though, then only she was going to know it. Wearing a bright smile, she approached the reception desk. 'My car hasn't. . .? Is there a message for me from a garage?' she changed her mind to rephrase it pleasantly to the man whom she'd seen many times before and who, from his broad welcoming smile, she knew had remembered her.

'I'm afraid not, Miss Kingsdale,' he apologised, and, as he passed a reservation card over to her to complete, Fabia, with her thoughts totally elsewhere, discovered that she was doing just that. 'How long will you be staying with us?' he queried when she handed him back the completed card.

'Er — just the one night, I think,' she replied, having hoped not to stay even that long but suddenly realising that, since she needed some kind of base where she could go to collect her thoughts, that perhaps to have a room where she could relax and think in private wasn't such a bad idea after all.

Her initial action on reaching her room, however, was to sit down by the telephone and to try and concentrate her attention on what she should do now. It was important that she ring her parents to let them know not to expect her that day. Against that though, if she rang the garage first, she would then have more of an idea of when she would be travelling back to England.

Opting to track down the garage first, Fabia crossed her fingers, and decided to enlist the help of the pleasant man on Reception. She reached for the phone, and had her hand actually on it when, before she had time to pick it up, it suddenly rang.

'Hello?' she enquired, and wouldn't have been at all surprised, the way her head was, had it been Reception ringing to say that she hadn't filled in her reservation form correctly. But, it wasn't the receptionist, but, the receptionist having put him straight through, it was Lubor Ondrus, Ven's secretary.

'Ah, I find you in!' he exclaimed for openers.

Fabia had no idea if Lubor knew that she had travelled to Prague with his employer last Sunday. But, since she had no wish to have a discussion with him about it when for all she knew he could have telephoned her hotel yesterday or the day before and been told simply that she wasn't available, she chose to assume that he did not know.

'How are you, Lubor?' she enquired brightly.

'Missing you, of course.' He didn't waste an opportunity to flirt.

'I'm sure you didn't ring me just to tell me that,' she replied, in no mood for light-hearted flirtation, try to pin on a brave face though she might.

'You're right, of course. Even though it always gives me pleasure to speak with you, I do have a purpose in phoning.' She did so hope that he wasn't going to invite her out, and was trying to think up some good off-putting excuse when, 'Your car has been delivered here, to Mr Gajdusek's home. I thought you might——'

'My car's *there*!' she exclaimed and, as it quickly sank in that she did not have to go chasing up the garage, or chasing over to somewhere near Františkovy Lázně either, she sent up a silent prayer that her luck *had* changed. 'I'll be up straight away!' she told Lubor and, 'Bye,' she ended the call whether he was ready to end it or not.

Seven minutes later, however, and, as Fabia slid into a taxi, her euphoria of the moment was over. Soon now she would leave Czechoslovakia, but she did not want to go. The taxi wound its way uphill, passing near the area where the colonnade stood—where the musical water fountain was—and as her heart began to ache afresh Fabia wanted more than anything to be there in May, when the fountain played.

But she wouldn't be here and, as the taxi went on ever upwards so Fabia tried to get herself in a frame of mind where she could deal cheerfully with Lubor's banter.

She was not feeling in the least cheerful however

when the taxi dropped her off at Ven's home. And, as soon as she had paid the driver and he had gone on his way she stood for some moments, looking at Ven's house, photographing it in her mind's eye because she knew—she would never come this way again.

Then suddenly she heard the sound of someone coming, and she put aside her sadness of heart, to realise that Lubor, perhaps on the lookout for her, must have spotted her from a window somewhere. Though before she could go round the side of the house to meet him, she saw that he had accidentally let Azor out too, for bounding round the corner, as he had one time before, came Ven's Dobermann.

'Azor!' she crooned, and, feeling a need to touch, to stroke the animal who had a part in Ven's life, she got down on her haunches to make a fuss of the dog. 'You'll be in trouble running out like that, you rascal,' she told Azor, giving him a friendly scratch on the top of his head.

She was still bent to the Dobermann when she discovered that she needed a moment to control a knot of emotion that came from the thought that she would see neither the dog nor its owner again.

Which was why she averted her head and kept it down when she heard Lubor come and stand close by. A second or so later, though, she felt she had herself under control, and with her head still down she flicked her glance to Lubor's feet.

Then Fabia knew herself wildly out of control. Because, as her heart started to thunder beneath her ribs, she realised that the last time she had seen those brown leather shoes, they were being worn by a man— in Prague!

Feeling certain that her imagination was playing tricks on her, Fabia, who knew that Ven was still in Prague, saw that it just had to be that Lubor owned an exactly identical pair of shoes.

She started to look up, past shoes to a pair of trousers the material of which she had last seen in Prague too! And suddenly, as an uproar began in her, Azor was forgotten, and she jerked to stand upright, and found she was looking straight up into a pair of dark smouldering eyes. Ven. . .was not in Prague!

She tried to speak but no sound would come. Then she found that she didn't have to say a word for, his expression the harshest she had ever seen it, Ven was wasting no further time, but was letting forth with a snarled, 'Just who the hell are you?'

'W-who. . .?' she stammered, while some part of her intelligence prodded away that—could it be that he somehow knew that she was not the person she was pretending to be? 'I—um—don't know what you mean,' she hedged.

And heartily wished she stayed quiet when, 'Like hell you don't!' he rounded on her. 'You certainly aren't any journalist named Cara Kingsdale!' he barked, and positively hurled at her, 'You owe me an explanation, *woman*! Start talking!'

Fabia had known all along that he would be furious if he ever found out. But, as she looked at him and witnessed that he was white with temper, so 'furious' seemed to be too mild a word. Oh, heaven help her— Fabia knew then that she was in deep, deep trouble!

CHAPTER NINE

HER heart going like a trip-hammer, Fabia fought valiantly to hold down panic. How much did he know—how much had he guessed? Had she somehow, inadvertently, slipped up badly somewhere? But there was no time for further speculation because Ven, his impatience plainly on a short tether, took a threatening step nearer, and hastily Fabia broke into speech,

'My n-name *is* Kingsdale!' she attempted to bluff it out just the same.

'You're sure of that, are you?' he slammed into her before she could draw another breath.

'Of course I'm sure!' she retaliated swiftly.

And promptly had the stuffing knocked straight out of her when, his aggression not letting up, 'You're sure your name's not Mrs Barnaby Stewart?' he grated—and Fabia's attempt to bluff it out promptly folded. She guessed it was pretty obvious that she had nothing to come back with when, his expression grimmer than ever, 'We'll finish this conversation inside,' he clipped, and although Fabia would by far have preferred that he simply hand over her car keys and let her go on her way, she realised that there were some responsibilities in life which you just couldn't duck.

Her happiness was at zero level as, owning that perhaps he had a right to an explanation, she went with him and Azor into the house. In the hall he gave the dog a command which saw Azor trot off somewhere, and then Ven was striding towards the drawing-room door.

'In here!' he commanded curtly, and held the door

open for her. There was nothing for it but for her to go in. 'Take a seat!' he rapped.

But she didn't want to take a seat. She wanted this over, and quickly. So she remained standing, and asked, 'How did you find out?'

'I'm the one asking the questions!' he shot her down in flames. And, while she was chewing on that, suddenly some fierce Czech expletive rent the air, then, '*Hell*, did you have me fooled!' he raged, and when she had been certain that his fury was wholly on account of her pretending to be a journalist when she was not, he proceeded to throw her thinking totally out of gear when, his face whiter than ever, 'You wanted that interview so badly you were even ready to commit adultery to get——'

'*Adultery*!' she broke in, feeling ill, and felt her own face lose what little colour she had. 'You're married!' she gasped.

'Not *me*!' he snarled. '*You*!'

'*I'm* not married!' she retorted, and for a few moments as her world righted itself and she realised that she must have momentarily got her wires crossed, because he had already told her he was not married, she realised too that, up until a moment ago, he must have thought *her*—Mrs Barnaby Stewart.

That much was most definitely borne out in Ven's next aggressive question of, 'Then just *who* the hell are you?'

It was a fair enough question, and when it came to being fair Fabia endorsed that she owed him this particular explanation. Not that, standing square in front of her, his expression brooking no refusal, he was giving her much choice.

She took a deep breath. 'My name is Fabia Kingsdale,' she told him. 'Cara Kingsdale—Mrs Barnaby Stewart—is my sister.'

Fabia was not sure what she expected after that.

Probably that Ven would go for her jugular in no uncertain fashion for the deception she had played on him. But to her amazement he did nothing of the kind, but, shaking his head as if he had been under some kind of stress, 'I didn't think I could have got your innocence so completely wrong,' he stated gruffly. And as colour started to return to his face. 'Your virginal shyness when we were in bed together. . .' he began to go on, but Fabia just wasn't ready for this conversation—she doubted that she ever would be. Though from the way she remembered it, she had been so eager to be his that shyness hadn't had a look in! But the fact that he must have discerned a certain shyness in her responses. . .

'Well,' she butted in fast, 'I'm not here to discuss such—er—such. . . I'm here only to collect my car.'

'Your car?'

'Yes. Didn't you know. Lubor telephoned. . .'

'It was on my instruction that he telephoned you,' Ven cut her off.

'I see,' she murmured, when she didn't see at all. But, feeling glad to have got him off the subject of how apparently her virginal innocence did not tie up with her being a married woman, 'Well, if you don't mind, I'll just collect my car and head back to England, and—'

'You've got one hell of a nerve, English miss, I'll say that for you!' Ven chopped her off stingingly before she could finish—and Fabia knew then that she wasn't going to get off as lightly as she'd hoped. In fact, knew it for certain when, 'Since you're not going anywhere for a while, perhaps you'd like to take a seat now,' he suggested.

It seemed a better idea this time. Her legs, she admitted, were feeling a bit rocky. She moved away from him and went over to the couch she had taken her ease in the last time she'd been in this room. But she wasn't feeling easy with him now, and as he pushed an easy-chair closer to her couch, and sat down opposite her, she had the uncanniest feeling that he wasn't going to let her out of the room until she had told him every last bit of what there was to tell.

Which, she privately admitted, was no more than was his due, seeing how, believing her to be someone else, he had wined her, dined her, housed her — Abruptly she shut her mind off. She would tell him all about her not being Cara Kingsdale, but, of the stupid idiot Fabia Kingsdale who had fallen head over heels in love with him, he would hear not a thing.

'I'm sorry,' she began. 'I know that doesn't and can't excuse the way I came here and attempted to pass myself off as Cara, but I've otherwise tried to keep to the truth, as far as possible.'

'You're twenty-two?'

'Yes.'

'A journalist?'

'No, I'm sorry,' she apologised again, and since she owed him, 'I work with my parents.'

'In Gloucestershire at their kennels and smallholding?' he questioned, causing her to warm to him that he had remembered so much.

'That's right. I suppose I'm a sort of kennel-maid — dogsbody. I'm sorry,' she said quickly again, 'that wasn't meant as a pun.' She halted, aware that she was gabbling. 'I'm nervous,' she explained.

'Of me? You have no need to be,' Ven assured her. And while she stared at him in some astonishment, 'I would never harm you,' he added.

'I — um — um don't think I thought you would. But — ' she stared at him with saucer-wide eyes ' — aren't you furious with me?'

'I was, but that was something else. . .' He broke off, and seemed to her strangely uncertain how to continue. And indeed, did not continue to tell her what that something else had been, but invited, 'Would you like to tell me how it came that, however badly, you attempted to impersonate your journalist sister?'

'Badly?' she queried. 'Was I so awful?'

'Dreadful,' he replied, and warmed her heart some more when a hint of a smile touched his mouth, and he voiced, 'Allow me to tell you, Miss Kingsdale, that your interviewing technique is appalling.'

'But—I never got started!' she protested.

'Exactly,' he replied. 'It is my experience of the journalistic fraternity that there is no question too intimate or too personal they will not stoop to. Nor any member of one's staff they will not intrude upon. Your sister, I feel sure, would never have wasted such opportunities as you had.'

'I've barely got the answers to any of the questions on my list,' Fabia had to own.

'You have a list?'

'A long one. Cara gave it to me. This interview means so much to her,' she explained in a hurry. 'We were all set to come to Czechoslovakia for her to see you and for us then to take a holiday while her husband was doing some work in America. Cara was then going to fly to America to have a holiday with her husband. But when I drove to London to collect her as we'd arranged, I found that she'd had a phone call less than an hour previously to say that Barney was ill. So naturally. . .'

'Naturally she flew to America to be with him,' Ven inserted, right there with her.

'I would have gone with her, but, as I said, the interview with you meant such a lot to her, she just couldn't cancel it—nor would she let anyone else— another journalist, I mean—do it for her.'

'So she selected you,' he put in quietly.

'I honestly didn't want to lie to you,' Fabia stated quickly. 'But with Barney being so ill, and with Cara being so upset, it made it seem awful that I wouldn't spend an hour of my life doing this one big thing for her.'

'So you agreed—even to the extent of using her name.'

'I didn't want to, honestly I didn't. But. . .'

'But love for your sister got the better of you?'

'Can you understand?' Fabia asked, her wide green eyes looking into his dark ones as she sought for his understanding.

'Yes,' he replied. 'From what I have learned of you, I would understand it less had you refused.'

'Oh,' she murmured, and wasn't at all sure how she felt about his reply. Wasn't at all sure that she wanted him to have learned anything about her that went to add up to what made her tick. 'Er—I know you said that you were the one asking the questions, and you've every right, of course,' she added hastily, 'but—hmm—when did you find out that I wasn't a journalist—that Cara was Mrs Barnaby Stewart. Can you tell me?'

'I don't see why I should,' he replied, but, to make her heart spurt, even though she knew that he meant nothing by it, 'But for you, I will,' he added. 'It was apparent from the start that, if you were a journalist, you were not of the hard-nosed variety.'

'I gave myself away?'

'You allowed me to deflect your questions far too easily,' he answered, 'Is it any wonder that from almost the first moment I saw you. . .' he paused '. . .I should start to be a little intrigued by you?'

'Oh,' Fabia murmured again. But she instructed her fast-beating heart not to be so idiotic, that Ven meant nothing by that other than that he was intrigued that her journalistic methods were unlike those of any other journalist he had met. 'Urm—so—hmm—how did you find out, about Cara being married?'

He shrugged. 'It was quite simple. I rang *Verity* magazine.'

Fabia's mouth fell open — she hadn't thought of that — though belatedly realised then that it was a fairly obvious thing for him to do. 'You wanted to authenticate that I was who I said I was?' she questioned.

But Ven was already shaking his head. 'Hardly,' he replied. 'you came well prepared with your sister's business card, and a letter typed on some of my headed paper.'

'But. . .' She thought her brain must be slowing up, because if he was certain at the start that she was who she said she was, why would he ring England? 'Why?' she just had to ask, 'when?' and, most oddly, felt a tension in the air that, for once, didn't emanate from her. Though what Ven had got to feel tense about she could not imagine, as she tossed out any such notion as absurd.

'When? Today. Why?' he repeated, and, giving her a long, level stare, 'Why — because you'd run away from me, that's why!' he stated with a hint of some of his old aggressiveness — or perhaps, Fabia suddenly wondered, startled, it was not aggression, but nervousness! Rubbish, she thought, and consigned that notion to the bin. 'Because I thought it a good idea to have your home address,' he added, in the same tone.

'Oh, I see,' she murmured, but all she really saw was that the question which had come to her — had he driven to Mariánské Lázně last night after he'd left her? — had been answered. Plainly, since he had been aware that she had 'run away' from him, he must have still been in Prague that morning, and must have returned to that hotel suite some time after she'd left. Which meant that he must have driven to Mariánské Lázně quite soon afterwards. But it was starting to worry her that he could so openly refer to her running away from him, and since she had no intention of going into the 'whys' and 'wherefores' of that, and since she had made her apology for deceiving him—and had got off rather lightly, she had to admit—Fabia got to her feet. Ven was on his feet too when she extended a hand and began, 'You've been very kind——'

'Kind!' Ven barked, her hand ignored as, his aggression once more out in full force, 'Where the hell do you think you're going?' he demanded.

Her hand fell back down to her side. 'Why—to England, of course,' she replied, striving with all she had to stay calm, 'My holiday is at an end now. In fact,' she went on when she could see that he didn't seem overly impressed, 'in fact, my parents are expecting me home today.'

'Sit down!' he snarled for an answer. 'You can phone them later.'

'Yes but——Look here——' she suddenly began to assert herself.

'Look here, *nothing*!' he chopped her off. 'I've not finished with you yet—not by a long way!'

'But. . .but you said—well, you intimated—no, s-said, I'm sure,' she stammered, not surprised that she was getting thoroughly mixed up, 'you said that you weren't furious with me any more.'

'I'm not—not about you pretending to be your sister. Not now I know. . .' He halted, and abruptly changed tack to demand, 'You're prepared to go back to England without that interview?' Oh, grief, Fabia fretted, and judged it better to stay quiet. But Ven, she discovered, was not prepared to let her off the hook, and, 'Why. . .' he began to challenge, '. . .when you're honest, I know it, yet have begun on a path of deception to one particular end—why, when it's so important to your sister whom—you love. . .' an alert look suddenly came to his eyes, and he broke off for a brief moment before continuing, his serious dark eyes holding hers '. . .a sister whom you'd do anything for, as you proved when you left England and came here — why are you ready to leave now, without another thought?'

No! Everything in Fabia cried out as she started to panic that Ven might yet hit on the truth of her love for him. Again she decided to stay quiet. But again, he wasn't letting it alone. 'What happened, Fabia?' he relentlessly pursued her for an answer. 'What has happened that is greater than your love for your sister, for you to break her trust in you.'

'Stop it!' Fabia cried, feeling torn in two.

But he wouldn't stop it, and, 'What is so large in your life that, when I've promised I would discuss an interview with you, you would prefer to leave before — '

But she had reached the end of her rope and couldn't take any more, and, speedily cutting him off. 'You don't consider being accused of being a "clinging" woman a good enough reason?' she hurtled in hotly.

'Oh, *moje milá*!' Ven exclaimed. 'I hurt you! I confess I meant to hurt your pride — but, oh, dear Fabia,' he said softly, and, his aggression all at once split asunder, he reached for her, took her in his arms, and gently cradled her to him.

It was heaven just to be in his arms, to lean against him, to breathe in his warmth, his fresh maleness. But she had been in his strong arms before, and as agitation at her own weakness assailed her, so, while she still could, she fought to be free.

Abruptly, at her first panicky push at him, Ven let her go. 'Thanks!' she snapped. 'But I don't need you to salve my pride. I can — '

'I didn't *want* to hurt your pride,' he stated. 'I *had* to.'

'Thanks again,' she retorted. 'Why you *had* to is a mystery to me, but don't do me any — '

'Don't you see — can't you remember how it was?' he asked, when everything was so indelibly imprinted on her mind that she knew she would never forget a moment of it. 'You were warm and giving in my arms until, in an understandable moment of shyness, you backed away. It was a moment when a stray thread of sledge-hammer sanity isolated itself and hit me, and I, in that scarce moment, knew that I had to protect you—from me!'

As swiftly as her anger had arrived, so it evaporated. 'From—you?' she asked uncomprehendingly, but was feeling in so much of a fog, she had to admit, 'I don't think I understand.'

'I'm not surprised,' Ven replied, and taking a long pull of breath, 'I don't seem to be doing this very well,' he stated, 'but at least we're talking—which makes it less difficult than I thought it was going to be.' And while, still in a fog, Fabia could only stare at him, he touched a hand to her arm and this time, instead of commanding her to 'sit down', he quietly asked, 'Would you be seated? Sit down and give me the time I need to explain everything to you?'

Fabia stared at him for a moment longer. She had thought he would wipe the floor with her if he ever learned of her deception. Yet here he was, his eyes steady on hers, with full knowledge of her deception— and *he* wanted to *explain* everything to *her*! Suddenly she was in no hurry to be anywhere but where she was. Suddenly too, as a kind of tension caught at her, she knew that while, because of her love for Ven, she could be on very shaky ground here, she must be brave, and stay no matter what, and hear him out. Because somehow—it seemed important!

Voluntarily then she moved back to the couch from which she had sprung up earlier. By the time she had sat down again, though, Ven had moved the chair he had used closer. And when he too sat down again, he was that much nearer—this time as though not meaning to miss any nuance of an expression that came over her face.

Be brave, she reminded herself, and kept her features composed when, 'Thank you, Fabia,' Ven began, and, seeming encouraged that she had stayed, 'To explain more fully why I found it necessary to be so brutal when you were such a delight. . .' He broke off, and, looking into her eyes, owned, 'I barely understood it myself then either. All I knew, in the heat of that moment, was that I had to protect you from me, had to take heed of that barely grasped truth that I couldn't perhaps take your virginity and then just walk away.'

'I would never have asked you for anything!' she protested proudly.

'Don't you think I knew that?'

'I never even thought of——'

'That was the trouble,' Ven cut in, 'neither of us *was* thinking. Up until that moment when shyness got to you, everything was happening naturally, with enchantment, with beauty, but with no thought of what consequences there might be.' Oh Ven, she wanted to cry— it had been like that for him too! 'Then there was I, fighting for control, and there you were wanting to come close again.' Fabia took that on the chin. 'I'm not Superman, my dear,' he made her bruised chin immediately better with that warm-sounding "my dear," 'so what else could I do—and I own that I wasn't thinking at all too clearly—but appeal to the pride I'd seen in you?'

'I was too—shocked to react at all initially,' she murmured.

'Oh, sweet Fabia, you've no idea what it cost me!' he applied more salve to her wounds. 'It was for you that I had to leave that hotel suite and not return until daylight.'

'You stayed away all night—because of me?'

'I begged a bed at my brother's place—a room just a

carpet away from you was much too close, the state I was in,' he confessed, and, while her pride recovered by leaps and bounds at his confession, 'Have you any idea, woman, what it did to me to return to that hotel to find you gone?'

She opened her mouth, and then closed it. And, as her heartbeats quickened, she was striving with all she knew to stay calm. Because it was quite obviously more than probable that all Ven meant by that last remark was that, having driven her to Prague, he felt it his responsibility to drive her back to Mariánské Lázně again.

'I — um — had a train to catch,' she offered by way of explanation.

'Train to catch! Not so much as a note did you leave for me!'

'You thought I should write — after what you said!' she exclaimed, while her heartbeats dully settled, for clearly he was more concerned with where the devil she had got to than with her in particular.

'Are you never going to forgive me for that?' he queried, and there was such bone-melting charm in him then that Fabia was glad that she was sitting down.

'Of course,' she replied evenly, and tried desperately to pin her thoughts on somewhere else. 'The receptionist at the hotel could have told you that I'd taken a taxi to Prague railway station,' she offered.

'She did,' he promptly revealed. 'But before my brain got into gear after finding you'd cleared the wardrobe in the lobby of your belongings and I realised you'd gone, I went through half a dozen possibilities before I rang Reception.'

Fabia blinked, 'You — did?' she enquired slowly, it never having dawned on her that Ven would be overly worried that she'd lit out.

'Of course!' he replied without hesitation. 'Had you gone to another hotel in Prague? I wondered. Doubtful.

Doubtful that you'd get in anywhere. Back to Mariánské Lázně, then? Or even the airport in Prague? I remembered then that you had some of your luggage in Mariánské Lázně. And what about your car? Surely you wouldn't go home without your car? But why would you go home to England without your car anyway?' Fabia saw no point in butting in to comment that she had in fact come very close to doing that very thing, and after a few moments' pause Ven went on, 'I knew I'd bruised your pride, but that had been necessary when my desire for you had threatened to blot out reason. But had I hurt your pride so badly that you'd leave for England — when you hadn't done your interview yet!' Fabia started to feel wary — he was close, too close to knowing that when hurt pride linked arms with hurt love, not a lot else mattered. But, to her intense relief, Ven did not pursue his thoughts in that direction, but continued, 'By my reckoning, be it a hire car back to Mariánské Lázně or a taxi to the airport, you'd most likely need aid from someone to help you with language difficulties.'

'So you rang Reception. I'm sorry,' she apologised, her action in not leaving a note seeming poor thanks now that she knew he had only been trying to protect her from himself when he'd called her clinging. 'I — er — didn't think at the time that you'd be that interested in — '

'Interested!' Ven exclaimed — and very nearly made her drop when he went on, 'One way and another, woman, I've been *interested* in you since I pulled up my car behind yours, and you batted those gorgeous green eyes at me and told me that your car wouldn't go.'

Gazing at him in astonishment, Fabia only just held down a gasp. 'Interested?' she queried huskily, and, trying desperately to get to grips with herself — he couldn't mean 'interested' interested, could be? — 'You mean, interested in me as a journalist?' she just *had* to find out more.

Ven looked at her levelly for all of one second, then, 'If you remember,' he answered, 'it was not until the next day that I knew that the beautiful green-eyed woman with stunning light gold hair *was* a "journalist".'

'Oh, y-yes,' she stammered, her heart suddenly finding a lot of extra energy. But, as she remembered her meeting with him that next day, she realised that she *must* be mistaken about his meaning of the word interest and the connotation she would like to put on it. 'I'm not sure what you mean,' she stated then, 'but you were most definitely hostile to me when you saw me the next day, and that was still *before* you knew I was a journalist.'

'I was alarmed when I saw Azor take hold of you. That in turn made me angry,' he explained. 'But, however it came across, I don't think I was feeling very hostile—how could I be when, since I knew which hotel you were in, I would probably have been in contact had you not arrived at my home.'

'You would?'

'I am certain of it,' he replied, but promptly settled her heartbeats to a dull, steady rhythm once more by adding, 'because of your car, didn't I have good reason to contact you?'

'Of course,' she murmured, and smiled to show that her heart had not just sunk down into her boots.

'But I had no need to use your car as a ploy, because there you were at my home. And even when I learned you were a prying journalist—and when I've always preferred my walks to be solitary—what do I find but that I'm asking if you would like to walk with me!'

Fabia felt then that if he went on in this 'lift her up, knock her down' fashion for very much longer, the way her heart was behaving, she would probably have heart failure. Though, remembering that walk with him, she recalled how happy she had felt, and she wondered if that had been when she had started to fall in love with him.

'It — er — was a nice walk,' she felt it would do no harm to comment.

'Nice!' Ven exclaimed, 'I've since realised that it was the beginning of the end for me!'

'I. . .' It was no good, her brain seemed like so much candy-floss. 'How?' she just had to ask for clarification.

'How?' he repeated, but, even though she thought that he suddenly seemed a little on edge, and although he appeared to hesitate — as if, most oddly, he was a little unsure, he then looked straight into her eyes and stated, 'There have been countless instances when, because of you, I've found myself doing things which I wouldn't have believed. Things which, to my mind have been totally illogical — and yet nothing on this earth would have stopped me from doing them.'

'Really?' she whispered, something in his look, something in the way he stretched forward across the small distance between them and reached for her hands causing her heart to race once more.

'Oh, yes,' he replied. 'Going back to that Monday — I had introduced my secretary to you and, up until the point where he asked if he could drive you back to your hotel, I hadn't given any thought as to how you would get back there.'

'You had to go out — you gave me a lift,' Fabia reminded him.

'I had nowhere pressing to go,' he countered. 'I invented having to go out on that instant. Purely, I know now, to prevent Lubor Ondrus from taking you.'

Fabia's mouth fell open. The feel of Ven's hands on hers, the touch of his skin against hers was making a nonsense of her thinking, but was he saying that he had been — jealous — of Lubor! Just a tiny bit? 'Oh,' she croaked.

'A very big "oh",' Ven murmured, and, seeming to take it favourably that she was not snatching her hands out of his clasp, 'What is happening to me, can I think, when I, who value my privacy and do not need an intrusive journalist in my home, find that I have done no less than invite you to my home for dinner?'

Fabia would very much have liked to know what indeed it was that was happening to him, but, her heart pounding, it was a question that she was afraid to ask in case the answer was another knock-down.

'I thought for a while, when you drove past Lubor and me at lunchtime the next day and looked so angry, that my dinner appointment with you might be off,' she felt safe in commenting.

'Angry? I was furious!' Ven informed her.

'Because you thought I'd been cross-examining him about you?'

'He has proved a better confidential secretary than to give revealing answers, despite his weakness for the opposite sex—however beautiful,' Ven replied. 'But, despite my perhaps allowing you to believe that, when you had the effrontery to talk incessantly about your lunch with him over dinner. . .'

'Incessantly?' Fabia queried in surprise, certain that she had never been so rude.

'It is the way it seemed to me,' Ven stated, but then qualified—and her heart started to thunder again, 'But then, until I met you, I'd never before experienced— jealousy.'

'Jealousy!' she gasped. 'You were jealous! Jealous of Lubor?' and didn't know where she was when, as if he didn't think much of sitting opposite her in one chair while she had the huge couch all to herself, Ven suddenly moved from his chair and came and sat down next to her on the couch.

Then, while her insides went into a tangle of mild uproar, he took hold of her by her arms—which in no way helped to mend the way she was feeling—and turned her to face him. And then it was that, with his eyes on hers, he solemnly confessed. 'Yes, jealous of Lubor Ondrus. Jealous, without admitting that gut-tearing feeling for what it was until recently.' Fabia was staring at him, struck dumb, when suddenly he let go one of her arms, placed an arm about her shoulders and, looking deeply into her eyes, said throatily 'My dear, dear, Fabia, cannot you see how it is for me?'

From somewhere, Fabia managed to find a voice of her own. 'I'm—not sure,' she answered on a whisper, as she strove with all she could find to keep her feet firmly on the ground because something too wonderful, too impossible, too impossibly wonderful was happening—wasn't it?

'Oh, *miláčku*,' he breathed, '*You're* not sure! Don't you know, can't you feel, how unsure *I* am? Please give me some hope,' he urged, 'because, apart from the certainty in my heart that *miluji tě*, I have never been so uncertain, so apprehensive at any time in my life.'

Fabia tried to speak, but her throat felt constricted. She was aware that she was trembling in his hold, but, when she suddenly realised that some of that trembling could be coming from Ven, only then did she realise the stress he was under, and, for him, she pushed through her own fear barrier.

She gave a small cough to clear the constriction, and even though her voice was husky, 'What does "*miláčku*" mean?' she asked.

'Darling,' he replied without hesitation, and, as her heart drummed a sudden staccato rhythm, Fabia pushed through another fear barrier.

'And "*miluji tě*"?' she enquired chokily.

Ven's answer was to cup a hand to the side of her face, and, with a wealth of sincerity in his look, 'I love you,' he translated quietly.

'Oh, Ven!' she cried, as tears sprang to her eyes.

'My darling!' he whispered hoarsely, and, as if trying to believe what her eyes were telling him, his arm tightened about her and, 'Are those tears, the ones you're only just managing to hold back, tears of joy?' he asked tensely.

'I love you too,' she replied simply.

They were the words he had been wanting to hear and with an exultant roar, and with both arms at once around her, he pulled her close up to him. His language was a mixture of Czechoslovakian and English then, as, '*Moje milá*, sweet *miláčku*, I love you so very much,' he cried, and cradled her against him, kissing her cheek, the corner of her left eye before, one of his hands moving to the back of her head, he adjusted her position until the skin of her cheek was against his. But, after a few seconds of delighting in the feel of her delicate skin on his, he pulled back, and never, as Fabia shyly looked into his dark eyes, had she seen such a joyous expression on a man. 'I can't believe it!' he cried, but held on to her firmly so that she had a very concrete impression that, if it happened that it was the truth, he had no intention of letting her go, not now. 'When?' he demanded.

In point of fact, Fabia could hardly believe it herself, but, 'Yesterday,' she answered, 'Yesterday, at the poet's statue,' she confessed softly.

'Sweet, lovely Fabia, my heart,' he cried, and gently, touched his lips to hers.

'Oh, Ven,' she whispered. And, with a hint of a smile coming to her mouth, 'When — for you?'

'I knew today, definitely. But it had been there, growing, there for me to see, had I but eyes.'

'You didn't want to be in l-love?' she asked shyly.

'It was outside my experience — I refused to recognise it. But it was there when my heart softened on witnessing the courtesy you showed my housekeeper, the smile you had for her; there when I asked you to dinner with no certainty why I'd done so, other than that it most assuredly wasn't on account of any interview. There, in the fact that, that same evening, when I can promise you that I've always been a most truthful man, I, to my own amazement, discovered that I was mouthing lies.'

'You've lied to me?' she enquired, not seeing how she could be offended when *she*, either outright or by implication, had told some whoppers.

'Forgive me, my darling,' he requested with such charm that she was ready to lie down and die for him. 'You'd asked about your car, and I told you that it could take a week or more for the garage to locate the part they needed.'

'But—that was untrue?'

'Your car had, late that morning, been delivered here,' he replied to her astonishment, and, while her eyes went huge in her face, 'It was, and still is, locked away in one of my outbuildings,' he added.

'B-but why?' she just had to ask. 'Why lie? Why couldn't you have. . .'

'Why couldn't I have told you?' She nodded. 'Why should I?' he replied with a hint of his old arrogance. 'Maybe I fully intended to tell you, but you'd made me furious by lunching with my secretary—jealousy again of course,' he inserted 'and then spent some of the mealtime telling me of it. And anyhow,' he ended with a trace of a grin, 'even though I wasn't admitting the power you had over me, I think that even then I subconsciously didn't want you driving off anywhere where I might not easily find you.'

'You wretch!' she exclaimed lovingly.

'Love me?'

'So much,' she whispered, and melted under his gaze, and then his head came nearer and, satisfyingly, his lips met hers.

'My pure angel,' he breathed raggedly when, quite some minutes later, he pulled back and looked down at her beautiful face, at her cheeks made pink by his kisses.

'Oh, Ven!' she sighed, and adored him when he bent and placed a tender kiss on her forehead.

'Is it any wonder that, while I might have been too hard-headed to accept what is happening to me, I could not deny I actually felt my heart give a tug that night?'

'When?'

'When — in this room after I'd finished telling you of the singing fountain, you said, "How lovely" and I own, I thought you the most lovely creature, in mind and body, that I had ever known.'

'Oh what a beautiful thing to say,' she sighed.

'I've told you only the truth, my lovely one,' he breathed, and this time Fabia raised her head and kissed him, then found that she was the one being kissed, so expertly too that when eventually Ven pulled back she was feeling on a totally different plane.

'Er — you've — hm — not told me any more lies, then?' she strove desperately hard to get herself back together, although from what she could see of it Ven wasn't objecting that his kisses had the power to scatter all sensible thought. 'Other than — um — the one about my car?' she managed a coherent sentence or two.

'Ah!' Ven uttered, and to her delight confessed, 'Well, there was that occasion when, after being disturbed by thoughts of you all night, I rang you at your hotel the next morning in the hope that I hadn't disturbed you.'

'That was last Thursday,' she remembered straight away.

'Right.'

'You had to drive to Karlovy Vary, and invited me along.'

'Wrong,' he replied, and, while Fabia stared at him with yet more amazement, 'I was impatient to talk to you, to see you,' he owned. 'When I saw Ivo with a parcel he was about to mail to his wife's cousin in Karlovy Vary, I told him I was driving that way, and that I'd drop it into the shop where Edita's cousin works if he wished.'

'But you'd got nothing to go to Karlovy Vary for?' she questioned wonderously.

'Not a thing, other than that you'd expressed a wish to go there, and I wanted to see you.'

'Did I mention that you're artful?'

'Did I mention that you're lovely?'

'Oh, Ven.'

Time ceased for a while for them as they kissed and held each other. Then Ven was pulling away from her. 'It — hmm — never was my intention to take you on the couch in my drawing-room,' he commented gruffly, purposely putting some daylight between them.

'I'm sorry,' she apologised breathlessly, so bemused by that time that she hadn't a clue what she was apologising for.

'I should think so,' he said severely, and paused, and swallowed as if he had some constriction, and then asked, 'Where were we? What were we talking about?'

Fabia loved that he seemed as befuddle-headed as she. 'Um — I vaguely remember something connected with Karlovy Vary.'

'Ah — yes. That was the morning — jealousy again — you outraged me by sharing coffee with me, and daring to mention another man,' he recollected. 'I knew then that my decision to send my secretary away on business was the right one.'

'You didn't send him away because of me?' she asked in amazement.

'You're damn right I did!' Ven replied forcefully and without apology. Though he did smile as he recalled, 'But our time together improved, did it not?'

'Oh, yes. It was wonderful,' she remembered. 'We had lunch at a place called Bečov and. . .'

'And when I'd parked the car I had an overwhelming urge to kiss you.'

'Honestly?' she gasped.

'Honestly,' he replied, and kissed her.

'Oh, Ven,' she sighed.

'Had you seen me then, as I left your hotel, when I gave into that need to kiss you — be it on the cheek, I'm sure you would have thought "poor Ven".'

'I would?'

He nodded, 'I cannot remember driving to my home. But as I left my car and started to go into the house it was then that I realised I was falling under the spell of this Englishwoman who had been such a delightful and charming companion that day.'

'Oh!' she breathed blissfully, and, with an impish smile turning up the corners of her mouth, 'Don't stop there.'

His grin was heart-turning to see, and he kissed her lightly on the end of her nose for her impudence. 'So there am I spending the rest of that day with you in my thoughts, and getting barely any rest from thoughts of you when I try to sleep at night either.'

'I'm sorry,' she apologised cheerfully.

'You look it,' he laughed, but continued. 'By morning I'd decided to take myself off to Prague.'

'Not because of me?' she asked amazed.

'Of course because of you!'

'But — why?'

'Why — because, though at any other time I could perhaps let my feelings have their head, this time, for a reason I simply wasn't seeing then, I just knew that it could not be like that with you.'

'Because of the interview?' Fabia guessed.

'To be very honest, *moje milá*. . .'

'What does "*moje milá*" mean?'

'My dear,' he translated for her.

'Thank you,' she murmured happily, and reminded him, 'you were being very honest.'

'To be very honest,' he repeated, 'it was of no consequence at all to me what you wrote in your interview. More important to me was the need to obey this instinct that warned me to put some distance between us.'

'You were — um — scared?'

'Why not? I'd never felt the strength of this emotion called love before. This emotion which, even as I planned to drive to Prague, while admitting only to liking you well enough to want to ease any problems that might arise, made me instruct Lubor. . .'

'What about my car?' she teased.

'That was different,' he told her grandly, and resumed, 'While ensuring that my secretary had enough work to keep him fully occupied for the whole of that weekend, and not really expecting you would have any need to contact him, I instructed Lubor Ondrus to give you any assistance you might require should a problem arise.'

'But qualified that it was to be on an impersonal basis only.'

'Ah,' Ven paused. 'I didn't think he'd tell you that. It was my jealousy at work again, of course,' he freely admitted.

'Oh, Ven, and I thought it was because you didn't trust me enough not to ask Lubor personal questions about you for my interview.'

'Sweet darling,' he murmured, and kissed all hurt she had felt away before, shaking his head, he said self-mockingly, 'And I thought that by taking myself off to Prague I might get you out of my thoughts.'

'But you didn't. Oh, you telephoned me the very next night from Prague,' she remembered, as too she remembered without difficulty, 'I thought you might have rung in connection with that wretched, abominable interview, but you were so bad-tempered. . .' She broke off when she saw one of his eyebrows ascend aloft. She realised at once that he could be forgiven if he reminded her that she hadn't been too sugary herself during that phone call: but he did nothing of the kind, though he did allow himself a small smirk before all trace of a smile went from him.

'And why wouldn't I be bad-tempered?' he asked. 'I'd telephoned you purely because I had a need to hear the sound of your voice and what do I get for giving in to such weakness? That voice I've missed wasting no time in telling me its owner had dined with my secretary the previous evening.'

'Oh, dear — jealousy?' she queried softly.

'Jealousy,' he admitted. 'And, if that wasn't enough, even while I'm realising what an idiot I'm being to grow so infuriated that you and Lubor Ondrus appear to be in each other's pockets, you, who have no fear whatsoever of my dog — indeed have that day taken him walking — now seem to be taking him over too! I decided it was time to return.'

'You come back for some papers.'

'I lied.'

'Oh!' she exclaimed open-mouthed, and as something else suddenly occurred to her, 'You wretch!' she berated him lovingly. 'You asked me if the garage had returned my car, when you'd got it under lock and key all the time!'

'You'd said you were thinking of going to Prague. To my way of thinking you had seen too much of my secretary, I decided on that instant that to take you out of his vicinity was an excellent idea.'

'You decided on the spot to come with me — to drive me to Prague.'

'Of course. And fell more and more in love with you, be it lunching with you, or dining with you, watching your innocent pleasure as you in turn watched the

astronomical clock strike the hour. When I kissed you
that first night, and accepted that I desired you, I knew
then that with the situation so volatile I should get us
both out of there and back to Mariánské Lázně.'

'But—you didn't.'

He shook his head. 'I thought I could handle it—but
the very next day we'd been sightseeing and returned
to our suite and I looked into your eyes and felt myself
drowning. The only way I could protect you was to
make myself scarce that evening.'

'You had an engagement, you said.'

'You've remembered everything?'

'I love you,' she said simply, and was warmly kissed
for her trouble.

'Oh, my dear heart,' Ven breathed, and held her
close up against him for long, long happy minutes.

'If it's any consolation,' she murmured contentedly a
minute or so later, 'I was pea-green with jealousy when
you went out that night.'

'You were?' he exclaimed, jerking his head back so
he could see into her face.

'I was,' she smiled. 'I denied it to myself, of course.'

'Of course,' Ven agreed. But to her delight, added,
'And I, of course, never had an engagement that
evening.'

'Truly?' she exclaimed.

'Truly,' he replied. 'I wanted to be with you but, for
love of you, had to go. Nor did I dare return until I
thought you'd be safely in bed, and no temptation to
me.' Speechlessly Fabia stared at him, and he went on
to explain, 'Then last night, after a sublime day, we
went out to dine and I began to admit to myself that
you were getting to me in a big way.'

'I thought you seemed a bit preoccupied,' she murmured happily.

'And I,' he replied, tapping a loving finger on the

end of her nose, 'thought you were a shade cool at times.'

'I'm sorry,' she apologised. 'In my defence, I'd only recently admitted to myself that I was in love with you. My conscience over that headache of an interview you'd promised Cara—and me making believe I was my sister—was really getting to me.'

'Oh, little love,' he breathed, and while from his adoring tone she knew herself forgiven, 'I—don't know quite how to tell you this——' He paused, but, clearly deciding that there was only one way, he proceeded to completely stagger her when, 'It is a fact, my dear, that I did not, and never have, promised an interview to your sister, or to anyone else representing *Verity* magazine.'

'Y-you—didn't?' she gasped.

'Had I done so, trust me, I would have been at my home that particular Friday to honour that promise.'

'B-but, but—Cara had a letter from you!' Fabia struggled to get her head together. 'She. . .'

'She received a letter from Milada Pankracova, signed by Milada Pankracova, but. . .'

'But you didn't dictate it to her!'

'I believe it was her last act before she left my employ.'

'You dismissed her,' Fabia remembered.

'Her work was not up to standard. Though it was when I heard her using bad language to my house-keeper and being unwarrantedly rude to Ivo that I decided I'd had enough of the woman.'

'You dismissed her on the spot.'

'I gave her an hour to clear out her desk. An hour, in which, knowing full well that I never gave interviews, she wrote to your sister, giving her an appointment.'

'Oh, heavens!' Fabia exclaimed. 'That wasn't a very nice thing to do.'

'And that is the biggest understatement I've heard.'

Ven smiled, giving her a loving look. 'Not only would she have put your sister to some considerable nuisance, for I would not have been able to see her had things gone according to schedule. . .'

'Because you went to Prague?'

'I wasn't scheduled to go to Prague then. According to my reckoning, I should have been giving my full and entire concentration to the final chapter of my work — a time when I would not, as Milada Pankracova knew, want any interruptions. What she didn't know, of course, was that I finished my work a few days ahead of that schedule, and was not here when you — in the guise of your sister,' he inserted gently, 'arrived.'

Fabia's eyes were wide with astonishment as she grasped what Ven was telling her. 'Are you saying that when I showed you Milada Pankracova's letter to Cara, that was the first you knew of any interview?' she asked, still feeling a shade staggered and needing a little more clarification.

'I'm afraid so,' he replied. But, before she could begin to feel at all mortified, 'Did I tell you how glad I am, heart and soul, that you came?'

'Oh, Ven,' she sighed. Though when some seconds later her brain began to function, 'So Lubor wasn't teasing when he seemed suprised that you'd agreed to an interview! He knew you hadn't.'

Ven nodded, 'When I got back from taking you back to your hotel that Monday, I instructed him to bring me all correspondence to and from *Verity* magazine. There was none.'

'Milada Pankracova had destroyed it?'

'So it appears.'

Lord, what a dreadful woman! 'But Lubor agreed that the interview was recorded in your diary,' Fabia suddenly remembered. 'He told me it had been over-looked, I'm sure he did!'

'Did I not say that he was a good secretary?' Ven

replied, the corners of his mouth picking up delight-
fully. 'His references spoke of his loyalty in the highest
terms.'

'Well!' she exclaimed, as she thought of all that had
happened through Milada Pankracova trying to make
things difficult for Ven. 'And there was I, in Prague,
thinking that you wouldn't discuss the interview then
and there because you were drained from working so
long without a break.'

'I have rapid powers of recovery,' Ven informed her
softly. 'Though, since Prague has reared its head again,
perhaps I should explain that, when we returned to our
hotel after dinner last night, with my feelings for you
seeming to be on an agitated boil, I had to invent
having someone to see.'

'Invent—you didn't. . .'

'I needed some time alone in which to get my head
together—you're very much of a distraction,' he
murmured.

'I'm glad, ' she replied impishly, though added, 'And
I went to bed, feeling unhappy and with a heavily laden
conscience and, for my sins, dreamt awful dreams of
you being in danger. I was still half asleep when I flew
into the sitting-room, to try to help you.'

'You wanted to help me!' he exclaimed in delight,
and just had to kiss her. But then avowed with a great
deal of feeling, 'I sorely needed somebody's help when,
with daylight I returned to that hotel and discovered
you'd taken a train back to Mariánské Lázně!'

'You—um—came after me,' she enquired politely.

'I think the term is—like a bat out of hell,' he replied.
'Even while then it still hadn't clicked in my brilliant
brain why I was acting so, I put my foot down, and kept
it there, and arrived here with about an hour to spare
before your train was due in. Trust it to be late, today
of all days!'

'You knew it was late? You telephoned the station?'

'The station, your hotel, England. I,' he declared, 'have been a mass of strain, tension and fear.'

Her eyes were large in her face as, 'Fear?' she queried.

'Fear that you might leave Czechoslovakia without first returning to your hotel,' he replied, then grinned wryly as he added, 'For the first time in my life I find that I can't think logically—for why would you take a train to Mariánské Lázně to leave Czechoslovakia, when you could more easily take a plane from Prague? Love, I've discovered,' he stated, 'does not recognise logic.'

'So you couldn't think logically,' she prompted, loving absolutely everything he was telling her, 'so. . .'

'So,' he took up, 'I then grew more and more agitated that, if you did leave, I didn't have your home address.'

'You would have contacted me in England?'

'Of course,' he replied unhesitatingly, making her heart sing. 'But, thank God, I didn't have to. Though I didn't know that then, so I rang your hotel—and, while insisting that they contact me, without letting you know, the moment you walked in. . .'

'You told them to phone you!' she gasped.

'Certainly I did,' he stated. 'And, at the same time, I demanded your address in England.'

'Heavens!' she exclaimed softly, only then gleaning some idea of how very stewed up he must have been.

'But they, incompetent fools as I then believed, gave me your address as somewhere in Gloucestershire, when I wanted your London home address.'

'I was about to be found out,' Fabia inserted.

'I was about to be even more demented,' Ven corrected. 'In my work it's second nature for me to double check all factual research. I then remembered Lubor's mention of having your business card on his desk.'

'Oh, dear. He still had it?'

'He still had it. Under the pretext of wanting to

return a pen which Cara Kingsdale had left behind
when she'd arrived to interview me, and which might
have sentimental value, I rang *Verity* magazine.'

'They gave you Cara's London address.'

'Not only that but, seeming very pleasant and eager
to please, I thought, the woman I spoke with then
suggested that rather than address my package to Cara
in her professional name, just to make sure the package
reached you, she'd better give me your married name.'

'Oh — help,' Fabia mumbled.

'You can look shame-faced. I went through hell!'
Ven gently scolded her. 'I was reeling with shock.
"Married!" I repeated — and, to cover my astonishment, found I was saying, "She doesn't look old enough
to be married". To which the friendly woman at the
other end remarked, "Cara would kill me for telling
you, but she'll be twenty-nine in August. I know,
because we share the same birthday".'

'I'd told you I was twenty-two,' Fabia popped in
quietly.

'You certainly weren't coming up to twenty-nine, I
was positive about that. But, with everything exploding
about me, I still hadn't got myself back together when
the message came from your hotel to say you'd just
checked in.'

'You. . .' Fabia began. But suddenly realised, 'You
got Lubor to ring and say that my car had been
delivered here!'

'I was in no state to speak to you myself! Have you
any idea, woman, how I felt waiting and watching for
your taxi to turn into the drive from a window upstairs?'

'You knew then that you loved me?'

'I knew, the moment I put the phone down from
making that call to England, that not only did I love you
with every breath of my being, but there was no way
that I could take your being married to anyone but me.'

'Oh!' she exclaimed, startled.

'You do love me, don't you?' Ven asked, his voice suddenly urgent.

'Yes, of course I do—so much,' she replied.

'See how you've got me.' He smiled tenderly. 'But then,' he excused, 'I've had but a short while to suspect—when you were prepared to leave without fulfilling your agreement to your sister whom you love so much—that you might, dare I believe it, be running from me because *you loved me* and had been badly hurt by my "clinging" accusation.'

'You're far too clever,' she whispered shakily.

'So put a clever man out of his misery, and tell me—are you going to marry me?'

'You're sure?' she asked, scarcely able to believe what he was asking.

'I've never been more certain of anything in my entire life. Marry me, Fabia,' he urged. 'Let me come to England with you, to see your parents, to give your sister that interview which brought you to me, and. . .'

'You're willing to let Cara interview you!'

'There is nothing I would not do for you,' he replied, and all at once frustrated beyond enduring, 'For pity's sake, woman,' he implored, and, reminding her of a comment she had made to him that delightful mealtime in Bečov, 'give me a straight answer to a straight question—are you going to marry me?'

'Oh, Ven, my darling,' she cried. 'Oh, yes.'

'At last! Thank you, dear love!' he declared fervently, and, as his head came down and he tenderly touched her mouth with his, 'We'll get married soon, *miláčku*,' he decreed. 'I can't wait long to have you warm and clinging in my arms—and mine!'

Welcome to Europe

PRAGUE — 'the golden gate to the heart of Europe'

Prague, the capital of Czechoslovakia, is superbly situated on seven hills, and offers a myriad delights to the visitor. The spirit of romance is everywhere — in the beauty of the varied architecture, the old-world atmosphere, the sparkling river and the peaceful parks and gardens. Wandering through Prague with your loved one, you can't help but feel the special magic of this charming city.

THE ROMANTIC PAST

Legend has it that Prague's founder was **Princess Libuše**, who saw the city when she was standing on a rocky precipice overlooking the **Vltava River**. Overwhelmed with inspiration, she stretched out her hand, declaring that she saw a great city whose glory would touch the stars. She dispatched her white horse to fetch a man called Přemsyl, and together they founded Prague.

Princess Libuše appears in another of Prague's legends. A beautiful woman, she had no shortage of lovers, but

184

when she grew tired with them it is said that she had them thrown from the Vyšehrad rock into the river!

The 'good king Wenceslas' of the famous carol is one of Czechoslovakia's most famous sons. **Václav** (Wenceslas) was assassinated while defending the Christian faith in the tenth century. Today his statue can be seen on an iron horse in **Wenceslas Square**, and it is claimed that he will awake to lead his people again in their time of greatest need.

One of the most famous sights in Prague is the **Charles Bridge**. The present bridge has been standing since the fourteenth century. Some claim that eggs were mixed with the mortar to give it durability! Others say that it has lasted for so long because its foundation stone was laid on the ninth of July, the day of Saturn's conjunction with the sun, which astronomers considered to be lucky.

Prague has been called a 'city of music'. The famous composer **Dvořák** was born in Prague, and Mozart made many visits to the city. He conducted *The Marriage of Figaro* here, and his opera *Don Giovanni* was premièred in Prague in 1787.

Mariánské Lázně, which is west of Prague, and where part of the story is set, was one of the favourite places of the poet **Goethe**. Mariánské Lázně's beauty inspired him to write his *Marienbader Elegie* for the young Ulrike von Levetzow here in the early nineteenth century, but sadly it didn't bring him luck — his love for her remained unfulfilled.

The **Vltava River** is associated with many romantic legends. If you believe in fairy-tales, why not go to look for the Czech water spirits, little men with green coats and pipes who have lived in the water forever? They are said to know every stone and every fish in the river, are very wise, and can always be relied upon to give you the right advice.

In 1989, after forty years of Communist rule, the communists were overthrown in the 'velvet' revolution, so called because not a single window was broken.

THE ROMANTIC PRESENT — pastimes for lovers. . .

One of Prague's most impressive sights is its castle. While you're there don't miss the imposing **St Vitus' Cathedral**. Even from the outside this huge, ornate building with its towering spires is overwhelming, while, inside, the stained-glass windows and the frescoes decorated with semi-precious stones are dazzling.

Before leaving the castle, take a wander down the romantically named **Golden Lane**, where there is a cluster of what are probably the tiniest houses you've ever seen. These houses are built into the castle walls and have been occupied by many craftsmen over the centuries.

Not far away from the castle is the **Malá Strana** area of Prague, the ideal place for a romantic stroll. It's a picturesque quarter with little winding streets, impressive churches and palaces, old houses and little taverns for refreshment.

And, talking of refreshment, it must be time for something to eat. . .Search out a *vinarny* (wine cellar) or *pivnice* (beer tavern) and settle down to a typically Czech meal. The food is extremely good value and draws on influences from the East, Hungary and Germany. It's not the place to be on a diet, though! **Dumplings** are traditional Czech fare and accompany many dishes, while for a starter you might like to try Prague's **ham**, which is hard to beat anywhere. And, to wash down your meal, **Czech beer** is famous worldwide. The best known brands are **Budvar** (the original Budweiser) and **Pkzensky Prazdroj** (the original pilsner).

Now you're refreshed, it's time to visit one of Prague's most famous landmarks — **Wenceslas Square**, with the statue of St Wenceslas on his horse. Confusingly, it is not actually a square at all, but a long boulevard. This is where people congregate at times of trouble, and where demonstrations begin. It is also the best place to shop — there are department stores and shops selling souvenirs such as antiques and folk art. But making your way round without giving in to the temptation of the alluring displays of the cake shops is almost impossible!

If music be the food of love, why not visit the **Mozart museum**? This villa was where Mozart stayed on his visits to Prague, and you can now wander through its rooms, which are restored almost to their original form. And while you wander through, you and your partner will be serenaded by the sound of his music.

Finally, don't miss a walk over what has become the symbol of Prague — the **Charles Bridge**. Walking hand in hand along this statue-lined bridge is an unforgettable experience whatever the time of day. In daylight you can see the sparkling river with its white swans, and the golden spires of churches on both sides of the river. Or you might prefer to wander across the bridge in the moonlight, when you'll be entertained by guitarists and street artists.

DID YOU KNOW THAT. . .?

* Czechoslovakia has a reputation for producing excellent tennis players. Recent stars include **Navratilova**, **Lendl** and **Mandlikova**.

* there are two languages in Czechoslovakia — **Czech** and **Slovak**.

* the way to say 'I love you' is '*Miluji tě*'.

* the man who invented the word 'robot', **Karel Capek**, was born in Czechoslovakia.

Accept 4 FREE Romances and 2 FREE gifts

FROM READER SERVICE

Here's an irresistible invitation from Mills & Boon. Please accept our offer of 4 FREE Romances, a CUDDLY TEDDY and a special MYSTERY GIFT! Then, if you choose, go on to enjoy 6 captivating Romances every month for just £1.80 each, postage and packing FREE. Plus our FREE Newsletter with author news, competitions and much more.

Send the coupon below to: Mills & Boon Reader Service, FREEPOST, PO Box 236, Croydon, Surrey CR9 9EL.

NO STAMP REQUIRED

Yes! Please rush me 4 FREE Romances and 2 FREE gifts! Please also reserve me a Reader Service subscription. If I decide to subscribe I can look forward to receiving 6 brand new Romances for just £10.80 each month, post and packing FREE. If I decide not to subscribe I shall write to you within 10 days - I can keep the free books and gifts whatever I choose. I may cancel or suspend my subscription at any time. I am over 18 years of age.

Ms/Mrs/Miss/Mr _____ EP55R

Address _____

_____

Postcode _____ Signature _____

mps
MAILING PREFERENCE SERVICE

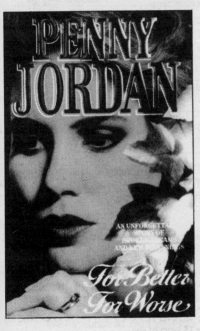

Next Month's Romances

Each month you can choose from a wide variety of romance with Mills & Boon. Below are the new titles to look out for next month, why not ask either Mills & Boon Reader Service or your Newsagent to reserve you a copy of the titles you want to buy — just tick the titles you would like and either post to Reader Service or take it to any Newsagent and ask them to order your books.

Please save me the following titles:	**Please tick**	√
UNWILLING MISTRESS	Lindsay Armstrong	
DARK HERITAGE	Emma Darcy	
WOUNDS OF PASSION	Charlotte Lamb	
LOST IN LOVE	Michelle Reid	
ORIGINAL SIN	Rosalie Ash	
SUDDEN FIRE	Elizabeth Oldfield	
THE BRIDE OF SANTA BARBARA	Angela Devine	
ISLAND OF SHELLS	Grace Green	
LOVE'S REVENGE	Mary Lyons	
MAKING MAGIC	Karen van der Zee	
OASIS OF THE HEART	Jessica Hart	
BUILD A DREAM	Quinn Wilder	
A BRIDE TO LOVE	Barbara McMahon	
A MAN CALLED TRAVERS	Brittany Young	
A CHILD CALLED MATTHEW	Sara Grant	
DANCE OF SEDUCTION	Vanessa Grant	

If you would like to order these books in addition to your regular subscription from Mills & Boon Reader Service please send £1.80 per title to: Mills & Boon Reader Service, Freepost, P.O. Box 236, Croydon, Surrey, CR9 9EL, quote your Subscriber No:.................................... (If applicable) and complete the name and address details below. Alternatively, these books are available from many local Newsagents including W.H.Smith, J.Menzies, Martins and other paperback stockists from 14 January 1994.

Name:...

Address:...

....Post Code:..........................

To Retailer: If you would like to stock M&B books please contact your regular book/magazine wholesaler for details.

You may be mailed with offers from other reputable companies as a result of this application. If you would rather not take advantage of these opportunities please tick box ☐